3/4/14

THE
MASON
JAR

Center Point
Large Print

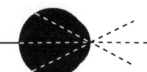

**This Large Print Book carries the
Seal of Approval of N.A.V.H.**

THE
MASON
JAR

*James Russell
Lingerfelt*

CENTER POINT LARGE PRINT
THORNDIKE, MAINE

This Center Point Large Print edition is published in the year 2014 by arrangement with the author.
Published in association with MacGregor Literary, Inc.

The text of this Large Print edition is unabridged.
In other aspects, this book may vary
from the original edition.
Printed in the United States of America
on permanent paper.
Set in 16-point Times New Roman type.

ISBN: 978-1-62899-005-8

Library of Congress Cataloging-in-Publication Data

Lingerfelt, James Russell.
The Mason jar / James Russell Lingerfelt. — Center Point Large Print edition.
pages cm
ISBN 978-1-62899-005-8 (library binding : alk. paper)
1. Grandparent and child—Fiction. 2. Letter writing—Fiction.
3. Large type books. I. Title.
PS3612.I5525M37 2014
813'.6—dc23
2013040690

Table of Contents

Mason jars were invented in the United States by Scottish farmer John Landis Mason in 1858. They were the prime method for preserving foods among most farmers and homemakers. The jars, molded with a threaded neck, accommodated a seal and tin lid for preserving fruits, vegetables, soups, jams, honey, and a host of other foods. Homes contained cupboards or storerooms with shelves full of Mason jars with their contents easily distinguishable.

However, when Americans left farms for cities after World War II, and refrigerators developed, Americans began freezing their foods. Today, Mason jars serve more as an icon of nostalgia, awakening fond memories of "helping Grand-mother and Granddaddy" prepare for family gatherings and reunions which always hosted an array of homemade sweet potato and pecan pies, watermelon, sweet tea, and jelly to garnish made-from-scratch biscuits.

PART I

Eden Hadley loved this place. It was her favorite pub in all of London.

The Dove pub overlooks the River Thames, just across the Hammersmith Bridge from London's city center. The sun would soon be setting over the water on this early autumn evening. White cranes pick at scrap food between the clefts in the cobblestone sidewalks, and gray street pigeons fight over crumbs along the terraces.

How could one not fall in love with London? A thriving city at the center of the world, whose nooks and crannies can still provide that village personality. Medieval towers are adjoined by chic buildings with glass windows as walls, like shimmering silver against the sun. Victorian Gothic cottages are painted in shades of chestnuts, tans, and blacks, all trimmed in white-washed frames.

Blossomed vines pour from flowerpots dangling below windows and above doors. Street lanterns, pubs, boutiques, and cafés line the streets and terraces where couples eat lunch and dogs wait tied to chairs. Boats painted in violets, greens, and crimsons, align the wobbly docks of the River Thames.

For a thirty-year-old girl from Colorado Springs

in 2016, living in London was magical. Eden came to The Dove every Friday, since she could take two hours for lunch. As a curator at Sotheby's, she knew the last shipment of art for the week came on Thursdays. Therefore, Fridays were spent bringing closure on the week and preparing for the next.

Tucking a lock of her hair behind her ear, Eden flipped to the next page in the book she was reading: Jane Austen's *Pride & Prejudice*. She had read the book at least fifty times but could never get enough of Elizabeth and Mr. Darcy. Would he truly save Elizabeth's family from that cunning and horrid Mr. Wickham? Would Elizabeth let go of her prejudice against Mr. Darcy and believe the words in his letter? And would Mr. Darcy abandon his pride and take Elizabeth into his arms?

Eden smiled and set her book down, allowing her imagination to replay her favorite scenes from the story. She lifted her velvety wine and took another sip as her gaze scanned the room.

The pub's dark, oak-planked floors looked as old as England. Coats of polish caked the floors and preserved the wood through the centuries. The day was a bit chilly and overcast, so the manager had built a fire beneath the mantle. The popping and snapping of the wood embers, and the flickering reflection of the flames against the walls, tables, and glasses somehow made London feel, well, comfy. Even the scents of burning wood took her back to her fireplace at home. If only she had a blanket to curl up in and never return to work.

A handful of older men sat across the pub at a square table playing Backgammon, eating sausage and mashed potatoes, and drinking pints of Guinness beer. Beside Eden's table, a younger couple sat in cushioned chairs. They were obviously on a first or second date, because their faces were bright. They couldn't look at each other without smiling.

They reminded her of her and Victor during their high school and early college years.

The bartender wore a white dress shirt tucked into his black slacks. He wiped the water stains from the glasses with a towel he kept draped across his shoulder, while talking and laughing with two older gentlemen. One wore a Knickerbocker hat, and the other, a vest and tweed coat. The bartender placed the glasses back onto their shelves. "What eva ya want, it's two pinds, lad," the bartender said with a smile.

"Doon't yaz call me a lad, pal," the old man in the vest said, grinning. He stood from his stool and shook his finger. "I'm olda and can still rlun cirlcles arlound ya."

Eden smiled at their accents. Though she had lived in England for over a year now, she still found the various British accents charming. *Whatever you want, it will cost two British pounds,* she interpreted. The older man must either be from Scotland or the northern countryside.

Her phone vibrated on the table. *Joanna* flashed on the screen. Eden's old college roommate from Pepperdine University.

"Hey, kiddo!" Eden said into her phone.

"Hey, lovely girl!" Joanna replied. "Are you going to Homecoming?"

"I haven't decided. Probably not."

"Are things better?"

"I still see Victor in every person's face."

"Well, I'm glad you finally got out of Colorado and away from that clinic. I know the work meant a lot to you. But time heals."

"I know."

"What about Finn?" Joanna asked.

"Clayton Fincannon? Joanna, that was ten years ago. I'm sure he hates me."

"No, he doesn't. And that's why I'm calling. Have you checked your mailbox?"

"No."

"I mailed you a book. A *New York Times* best-seller. *The Mason Jar*. Ever heard of it?"

"Yeah," Eden answered, "but I haven't read it."

"Finn wrote it."

"What?!" Eden almost tipped over her glass.

"Yeah. And it's intense." Joanna was laughing now. "It's beautiful, Eden. It really is. He says wonderful things about you, lovely things. I even cried a few times. I loved it. I really did. I know

14

it's about you. It's got to be about you. I mean, Finn didn't date anybody else at Pepperdine. He changes your last name but it sounds like you all the way through. He gives you the name 'Eden Valmont.'"

"Valmont?"

"Yep."

"Why?"

"To protect your identity, probably."

"What's it about?"

"Your time together at Pepperdine," Joanna replied. "The book was published last year, it seems."

"You sent me a copy?"

"Yeah. It should already be there."

"Wait, how did you get it?" Eden asked.

"Ryan sent it to me."

"Oh, no," Eden moaned. What had Finn written about her?

"Eden," Joanna said, her voice softening. "Finn loved you. You needn't worry."

"What does he say?"

"You just need to read it. That's all I can say. I need to let you go, but we'll talk later."

"Okay."

"Oh! One more thing," Joanna said. "Ryan said Finn might be at Homecoming."

Eden remained quiet on the other end, thoughts tumbling through her mind. She couldn't even remember when she'd last thought of Clayton

Fincannon. It was so long ago. The last she'd heard, he was living in Africa, working with street orphans.

"Are you still there?" Joanna asked.

"Yeah." Not once had she returned for a homecoming. And now, if she did attend this one event, her entire life could completely change.

"Well," Joanna continued, "just letting you know. It'll be good to see you! We'll talk later, okay?"

"Okay."

Clayton Fincannon, Eden thought to herself. Images played in front of her eyes like an old movie reel, memories of Finn, with his soft, brown hair and shy smile. She saw him stirring the honey and milk into their hot tea at Dietrich's Coffee in Malibu. Finn looked over and smiled at her, his hazel eyes shining. He kissed her temple, and she remembered blushing. Warm feelings had swept through her body like an ocean wave. But it was over, she thought, bringing herself back to attention. That was a long time ago.

The next day at the museum, Eden's colleagues were concerned. "You seem distracted," one lady remarked. Eden gave excuses about deadlines, reviews, and feelings of stress. But secretly, she was nervous about what she might read in Finn's book. Her brief time with Finn had been lovely, but she couldn't recall many details of those days together or even what they had talked about. She had hurt him, she knew that. She had never set out to intentionally hurt anyone. She feared Finn might seek retribution through his writings. But Finn wasn't like that, was he? Not that she could remember. And besides, Joanna said the book was lovely.

Eden found herself bobbing her knees up and down while sitting behind her desk, and picking and biting her nails while at home. Eden lived in a flat in Notting Hill with a roommate. Even her roommate asked Eden why she was so quiet and nervous, but Eden shrugged and made excuses about work.

When she returned home after dinner with friends, she found a package from Malibu awaiting her on the kitchen table. She dropped her purse onto the table and lifted the box. Maybe she needed to put on some tea before she opened this.

Eden walked to the jars of various teas sitting on the kitchen counter. She scooped out a generous helping of English Breakfast, which she purchased at the farmer's market. After dropping the tea leaves into the filter basket on the coffee maker, she turned on the water. She removed a mug from the cupboard and mixed the freshly brewed tea with milk and honey, remembering Finn again.

She picked up the package, pulled a knife from the drawer, and cut through the tape. Opening the box, a sticky note was pasted to the front cover of a book. "Here you go, love," was scribbled in Joanna's handwriting.

And there it was. *The Mason Jar* by Clayton Fincannon.

Eden took her mug into her hands, slipped off her shoes at the edge of the living room rug and pushed them aside with her feet. A reprint of Van Gogh's *Café Terrace at Night* hung on the wall, across from Caravaggio's self-portrait, which he painted while living in Italy during the sixteenth-century.

Her flat's living-room window overlooked the city center. Streaks of pinks and purples painted the western sky, and reminded Eden that nightfall approached.

She sank into the soft cushions on her couch, and opened the front cover of Finn's book.

THE
MASON
JAR

Everyone has a moment in history, which belongs particularly to him. It is the moment when his emotions achieve their most powerful sway over him, and afterward when you say to this person, 'the world today' or 'life' or 'reality' he will assume that you mean this moment, even if it is fifty years past. The world, through his unleashed emotions, imprinted itself upon him, and he carries the stamp of that passing moment forever.

—John Knowles. *A Separate Peace*

Chapter 1

"You know, Finn," Grandpa said. "All your life you've shown your desire to learn from others. You've always looked for people with a life full of experiences, knowledge beyond yours, to help guide you. When you couldn't learn anymore from someone, you moved to another. I know some of your mentors didn't always say the right words you needed to hear at the time. But, I'm glad you sought them. Now that you understand what happened and why, you can listen to the inner voice telling you your vocation, the things you can use your talents for to better the world before you leave it. You are no longer running from the world and all that has happened. You are moving toward something new, and you now have the experience to know the difference."

I remember that sunny, autumn afternoon. I had just returned from Africa, after five years of working with street orphans in Nairobi. Grandpa and I were sitting on his front porch in Tennessee, rocking back and forth in the rocking chairs he built. The leaves were auburn, fiery red, and a sugar-yellow. Their scent drifted through every light breeze to fill our noses as we sat and sipped the sweet tea from our Mason jars. Every time I sat with Grandpa and held a jar of tea in my hand, I was reminded of the old Mason jar on his cherry-oak desk in his study, where we still left letters for each other. Letter writing, though seldom it had become, was still a tradition we had kept since I was a boy. Over the years my letters were always confessions or questions. His were words of advice and affirmation of the good qualities he saw in me. When I grew older, we wrote more from sentiment.

When he wasn't working in the garden or re-filling the hummingbird feeders, he might be in his study, where bookshelves and floors were polished with *Old English* wood conditioner, a dark brown finish that made his entire home look like something out of an old Oxford painting. His study, always tidy, was filled with the scent of books and his occasional tobacco. The stories in his books were as old as *The Epic of Gilgamesh*, and his bookcase was filled with works by poets and philosophers dating back to the Classical period.

I knew when Grandpa had been reading, because he always ended his quiet time with a smoke from his pipe while his mind digested the author's words. He stocked his pipe while sitting in his leather, swivel chair, which spun around behind his desk. Then he would walk outside and light his pipe during a stroll or while sitting beside the fire pit on his back porch. The smoke's sweetness, of vanillas and black cherries, clung to his neck, hair and hands, an inviting residue.

I outgrew many mentors as life progressed, but never Grandpa. Each time we visited, I walked away taking deep, soothing breaths with weight-free shoulders. Some of his quotes to me are like a poster hanging on my bedroom wall, photographed in my mind:

To gain life, you must first sacrifice it.

If you want something too badly, you often lose it.

Never make philosophy your master— only your mistress.

The finite will never understand the Infinite, so stop trying.

Sometimes the greatest love we can show someone is to just let them be.

Grandpa helped raise my older brother, Caleb, and me. He was a devout Christian, so devout and faithful he often got on our nerves. But we were taught to respect God and love Him by loving and respecting ourselves and others; to recycle and take care of the planet, for it was our home; to have the wisdom to never lose control of ourselves by giving in to anger or alcohol; to stay away from drugs and not to engage in sex outside marriage. He always claimed following such advice would save us from a "plethora of problems."

He was the gentlest man I ever knew. He always smiled that grandfather smile, the one with crow's feet beside his eyes and dimples at his cheeks. He patted my back, spoke gentle words of comfort and acceptance, and offered love without conditions. All kids need a man like that in their life, a man to whom you can tell anything and who won't ridicule or mock you. An honest man who can look at you and say, "I believe you have what it takes."

"I don't think I'm still in love with her," I answered him, continuing the conversation we had begun before. "But I never loved a woman before I met her, and I haven't loved a woman since. I wonder if that's it. You know, if she was the one, but I lost her."

"But God doesn't work like that," Grandpa replied. "He doesn't plop a girl down and say, 'Okay, it's this one or no one.' Mates die all the time and people remarry. Sometimes, people marry prematurely or under false impressions and they later divorce. And we're to say to them, 'Well, too bad'? I don't think so.

"You know, Finn, you see everything from the younger side of thirty. I see in hindsight from the other. You might live another fifty or sixty years. If you live until your eighties, like me, that means you still have another lifetime in you. So live your life with passion. There's a lot to see and do in this world. You just be the kind of man you know God wants you to be and the right girl will find you."

But I thought she had been the right girl. Eden Valmont. That was her name. Valmont pronounced *Val móne* with the *o* emphasized. Very French. Eden's Italian black, silky hair and almond eyes turned young men's heads. She walked with her shoulders upright, crossed her legs when she sat, and the tone in which she spoke was wrapped in warmth and brightened with eloquence.

When she looked into my eyes, a passionate radiance overtook hers, and flames burned within them. Her passion of life and for love was like an ocean I wanted to sink into.

Our time together was during our college years at Pepperdine University in Southern California, where I attended graduate school. Pepperdine, with its Mediterranian architecture, its seashell-white buildings and red-clay roofs, which glow gold at sunset, overlooks the coast in Malibu. Pepperdine's green lawns end at the beach, and blue waves crash against the sand, the sound echoing across campus.

Bees, butterflies, and hummingbirds fly between the endless flowers bordering the walkways and filling the curb corners. Every building, apartment, and dorm has an ocean view. *The*

Princeton Review named it the nation's most beautiful college campus, and it stands within twenty miles of Los Angeles, Santa Monica, Venice Beach and Beverly Hills.

I played lacrosse at Pepperdine, even though I was a graduate student. I still had two years of eligibility and I missed the action and competition. Since Pepperdine is built on plateaus in the hills, like stepping stones for giants, most points allow a magnificent view of the ocean. From the soccer and lacrosse field, the ocean and palm trees provide the backdrop, and loose balls that tumble off the side seem lost at sea. After a final practice game, celebrating a winning season, we removed our gear on the sidelines as the dew began to settle on the field and the scent of cut, wet grass, filled our noses.

I had removed my helmet and I remember laughing at a joke someone had made, when I saw Eden for the first time. She wore a Pepperdine sweatshirt and shorts and stood on the opposite side of the field, talking with friends. I must have gone into a trance because Ryan hung his arm around me. "Like what you see?"

Ryan was a like a brother to me. Slender and my height, he often stuttered when he spoke and he suffered from asthma. He had dark hair and eyes and wore black-rimmed glasses. Coming from Canada, he loved hockey but freed himself to watch all my lacrosse games.

"Who is that?" I asked. Fellow students passed by and congratulated me on our win.

"Eden Valmont," Ryan said. "Joanna's new roommate. Joanna loves her. She just transferred from Colorado and use to work with street orphans in Italy."

"Is that right," I muttered.

"She has a tender heart, Finn," Joanna said, having arrived at Ryan's side. "Be careful." Joanna had worked with inner-city children in New York every summer, and like Grandpa always said, you know a lot about people by who their companions are. And you can trust them when they vouch for people they know.

Katie Wilson was looking back and forth between Eden and I and scowling. Katie was an attractive blonde with hazy, sky-blue eyes and always dressed in a preppy style. And she followed Joanna around, a lot.

One of my lacrosse brothers and friend, Brian "Oz" Bailey, also stood nearby. He loathed Katie because she was a sorority girl. Oz hated frat boys too. Being from Tuscaloosa, the home of the University of Alabama, he had had terrible experiences with the "Greek culture" (slang for sororities and fraternities). I've never been to Tuscaloosa, but from what I gather, the Greeks have created a very exclusive culture there. Sort of like *Animal House*.

Oz sported a shaved head and always wore a

black t-shirt, even under his lacrosse jersey. He was an MMA fighter. Cage fighting, Ultimate Fighting Championship, you get the picture. Oz was an interesting guy. He came from a poor family and got in trouble with the local sheriff when he was a kid. So, his chances of winning a grant or scholarship were ruined.

He heard about the Os Guinness Scholarship (pronounced "Oz"), which offered free tuition to anyone from Ireland who wanted to study theology at Pepperdine. So, Oz flew to Ireland, learned the Irish accent, and mailed in forged documents from Dublin. Oz was accepted, so he spoke with the Irish accent, just in case an administrator stood nearby. That's how he earned the nickname, Oz.

Oz overheard our conversation, stepped between Ryan and I, and remarked, "Finn, didn't you say once that you don't date because girls are shallow or mean?"

"Most girls," was my response. "Besides, if you saw the drama my friends went through in high school and college, you'd vow not to date until you're thirty, when everyone's a bit more mature."

Oz threw his head back and laughed. "I don't blame ya, Finn. You've just described every sorority girl at Pepperdine."

"We're not all like that!" Joanna said, slapping Oz's arm.

"Ow!" he yelled, jerking his arm back with an exaggerated expression.

When I returned my attention to Eden, J.J., a handsome, bleached-blond kid, was flirting with her. She crossed her arms and seldom made eye contact with him. I hoped she wasn't interested.

"What's J.J. doing?" Oz growled. "Frat beach boy."

Oz jogged over to Coach Sparks, our lacrosse coach, and told him that J.J. was bragging earlier that he planned to keep his lacrosse helmet since he's a senior. "He plans to ship it home tomorrow," Oz told him. Now of course, none of that was true. But Oz couldn't stand J.J. because he was in a fraternity. J.J. also played water polo and was originally from California. These facts coupled with his bleached hair . . . all the more reasons for Oz to hate the guy.

"Don't tell him I told you," Oz said to Coach, and then jogged back to our group.

"J.J.!" Coach Sparks yelled. "Get your butt over here!"

I dropped a ball in my lacrosse net and launched it to Eden's feet. Then I proceeded to fetch it.

"Finn!" Ryan said quickly and nodded over his shoulder.

My professor and mentor, Dr. Daniels, was waiting for me. He became a personal friend to me during those years. A professor of literature, he had served in humanitarian work in South America for nine years. Now he spent his summers leading students on local and foreign humanitarian projects. He was in his fifties with all four of his kids in college, and he was the most energetic man I knew.

"Hey, Doc," I said, skipping over, and shaking his hand.

"Good job out there."

"Thanks."

"We have a special guest at the banquet tonight. Chaplain Metcalf."

"Chaplain Metcalf?" I said, with a raised brow.

"Yep. He's leading the opening prayer and wants to meet you."

"Me?" I asked, astonished.

"He's impressed with your work," he said, smiling. "I've told him a lot about you."

"Thank you," I said. And I meant it. "He's an incredible leader."

"Well, I'll see you at the dinner."

When I turned back around, Joanna handed me the lacrosse ball. And Eden stood beside her.

Once our eyes met, they explored each other's with tenderness. I knew when I looked into those eyes that I could love her for the rest of my life. Intoxicating and lovely, her shining black hair lay like a groomed mane across her shoulders.

"I think you dropped this," Joanna said, presenting my ball to me with her tongue in her cheek.

"I did," I replied, pretending my clumsiness was to blame. "Thanks."

"I'm Finn," I said to Eden, stretching out my hand.

"Eden," she said and shook it.

"I've never met a girl with that name before. It's lovely."

"Thank you." She averted her eyes and bit back a smile. Shy? Now I liked her even more.

"Do you like J.J.?" Oz blurted out.

"Who?" Eden answered.

"Mr. frat boy over there."

"No. I—"

"Good," Oz interjected. "Because he'll give you an STD."

"Jo," Ryan said, handing her a camera. "Will you take our picture?" Ryan motioned Oz and I to join him.

"You guys stand together," Joanna said, adjusting the sights on the camera. When she took the picture, Ryan and Oz snatched the camera and reviewed its quality.

"Nice," Oz said.

"So, are you guys going to the dinner?"

"Wouldn't miss it," Ryan said.

"Eden?" Joanna asked her new roommate.

"I have to study," Eden answered. "Besides, I hear the speakers are usually boring."

"They're new every year," I said, biting the corner of my lip.

"Finn's this year's speaker," Joanna added, chuckling.

Eden blushed.

"Maybe you shouldn't come," I told her, grinning. "I'd hate to disappoint you."

Eden chuckled and shook her head, her face still cherry-red.

Katie jumped between us. "Hi, Finn."

"Hi, Katie." I glanced at Oz, who rolled his eyes at me. "You played good," she continued, bouncing on her tiptoes.

"Thanks."

"After dinner," Joanna said, "we're going to Santa Monica."

"Come, Finn," Katie added, cocking her chin and smiling at me. Then she touched my arm. "We can ride the Ferris wheel."

"Okay." I wasn't going to be rude to her. She had never mistreated me. But I didn't trust her, either. She seemed manipulative. And she always wore some expensive designer perfume that reminded me of grandmothers.

A semester earlier, Katie had asked me to be her date at a sorority ball. Though I'm not against dressing in tuxedos and escorting charming women, I could barely afford the clothes I wore. I was poor by SoCal standards (slang for Southern California). Pepperdine awarded me a full tuition scholarship because I served in humanitarian work in Europe and North Africa. My ambitions were to serve as a professor, and take students with me on humanitarian projects during the summers. An inner richness is all I sought and cared about.

We gathered our lacrosse gear and Katie slid her arm in mine as we left the field. I glanced back over my shoulder, at Eden, but she was talking with other friends. When my eyes landed back on Katie, she was staring daggers into Eden's back.

Students filled Pepperdine's cafeteria that night for the 2006 Project Serve Dinner. Flowers decorated white-clothed tables. Grilled asparagus, mashed potatoes, and roasted chicken or veal was served to those who had paid their money in advance and reserved a table. The guest speakers were seated on a stage, and a banner was strung behind us listing all the cities Pepperdine students would volunteer in during spring break. Ryan, Oz, Joanna, Katie, Eden, and a group of our classmates shared a table with a seat left open for me between Ryan and Oz. Those gathered on stage included Dr. Daniels, Chaplain Metcalf, Pepperdine's Chancelor, and our university president, Dr. Benton.

"Instead of giving handouts to people," I said, concluding my speech from the podium, "we must seek ways to develop a system where people work and thus receive financial help from members of their own communities. Trying to help people, if not done responsibly, can cause hurt. The answer is not to grow bitter and quit when things don't work out as we imagined, but to reassess and try again. As my grandfather once said, failure isn't failure. Failure is realizing what doesn't work. As we go, may we remember Pepperdine's motto: Freely give as you have freely received."

I knew something had to change in the way we conducted service projects. I had seen too many good intentions hurt too many people.

When I finished my talk, everyone clapped, and those on stage congratulated me. Chaplain Metcalf had served in the Iraqi war and founded a veterans' clinic in Colorado. He was a hero not only to the veterans, but to those at Pepperdine as well. He visited and spoke at our school on a regular basis. Tall, broad-shouldered, with sandy-blond hair, his presence commanded respect, but he spoke and acted with the utmost humility. I admired him.

"You know," Chaplain Metcalf said, shaking my hand. "I've heard a great deal about you."

"And I have you," I answered. "Especially your work with the soldiers."

"You know, when we first opened the clinic, Pepperdine students were the first to volunteer. And I heard you're the reason for that."

"You're the reason," I told him. "You opened the clinic."

"Not only are we treating soldiers with PTSD, but also with depression and war injuries. Now we have a staff of full-time nurses."

"Well, let us know if there's more we can do," I said. Then we shook hands and I joined my friends at our table. Members of the school catering team delivered chocolate or vanilla cake with coffee to those seated.

"There he is," Oz announced, patting the chair. "The professor."

"I'm not a professor yet," I answered, smiling at him.

"No, but you will be."

I grabbed my seat and looked back at the stage. And for some reason, Chaplain Metcalf was still watching me.

"So, as I was saying," Oz began, "I speak English but do terrible in English class." Those gathered around the table laughed.

"What are you guys reading now?" asked Joanna.

"*Pride & Prejudice*," he answered.

"I love that book."

"I never really liked Mr. Darcy, though," I said. Eden, who had previously been staring off to the side, daydreaming, shot her eyes at me.

"Why?" she asked. I sensed an offense brewing, but I couldn't help myself.

"He was rude to the commoners," I said, defending my position.

"When?"

"At the ball. In the beginning."

"But we find out later that he wasn't like that," she replied.

"But he was," I argued.

Eden forced a smile. "But Jane Austen had to

introduce him that way. We had to see him in the beginning, through Elizabeth's eyes. That way, we don't blame her for hating him. That sets up the entire story."

"I just think she could have written it differently."

"Well, how would you have written it?" she snapped.

"I would have stated later in the novel that Mr. Darcy had bumped into Mr. Wickham, outside, before the ball. And they had an argument or a fight. And that's why Mr. Darcy entered acting sour."

"You do realize Jane Austen's one of the greatest writers of modern history."

I should have stopped but again, I just couldn't help myself. "She's just a girl."

The blood rushed to Eden's face. I returned my attention to Oz and Ryan and pretended that I had made an offhand remark. I could feel the heat from her fuming.

"Just stay away from him," I heard Katie mumble to her. "Can we please not talk about class?" she exclaimed, addressing the group.

"Yes. Good idea," Ryan said.

A freshman visited our table to speak with me. He wanted to share with me Habitat for Humanity's business model. I stood and shook his hand. So, some days later, Joanna recounted that she had leaned over to Eden and whispered,

"Finn's a handful isn't he?"

"He's arrogant," Eden had responded.

"No," Joanna replied. "You just have to get to know him. He's a great guy."

It's good to have girls who'll vouch for you.

Later that night at the Santa Monica pier, the roller coaster, Ferris wheel, bumper cars, and various carnival rides lit the sky.

The sparkling carnival lights of pinks, oranges, and purples hold a promise of everything that evokes excitement for an inner child. There, couples walk hand in hand eating hotdogs and cotton candy. Scents of fresh funnel cakes and powdered donuts fill the air. Children chase each other with balloons and sparklers. Vendors pace in front of their booths, pitching deals to bystanders.

The pier remains open for most of the night. You'll recognize it from pictures in magazines and from films, since anyone who needs a fair to film and photograph has access to one year-round. A quaint, rustic pub called Rusty's unites all on the pier. There, a beach bum with a pint of stout will sit two seats away from high-class women sipping Napa Valley wines. On stage, men wearing vintage clothing might play a guitar or a trumpet. Depending on the band playing that night, younger music lovers might form a mosh pit. Musicians and entertainers range from Mandy Moore to that guy you see reviewing sheet notes at the coffee shop.

That night at the pier, the girls and guys separated into their groups; normal behavior when you're young. But Eden and I watched each other.

Katie stepped in front of Eden and engaged her in conversation. And I wondered if she had been eyeing us again.

Oz drank spiked cola from a paper cup. He usually carried a flask of whiskey in his pocket. He offered some to me but I waved it away. Oz smiled at me wryly and tipped his flask over his cola, emptying it. I chuckled at him. He had learned a long time ago that he wouldn't get much of a response from me during his agitations. That was something about Oz. Sometimes he said and did things just to watch people's reactions. Ryan wasn't too fond of him. Come to think of it, most people weren't too fond of Oz. But I think it's because people didn't understand him. They didn't take time to.

When some of our friends shouted that they were all going for yogurt, they started to fill their cars. Eden and I held back, hoping to ride together. Ryan drove a green Camaro convertible and others loaded into trendy cars and jeeps. Joanna sat in the front seat of Ryan's car and Oz sat beside Katie in the back. Not his first choice, or hers. A spot was open next to Oz, and only a spot was left in the jeep behind us. Katie had chosen Ryan's car, I presumed, believing I would ride home with Ryan and Oz.

"Listen, Katie," Oz said, "why don't you ride in the other car and let Finn and Eden sit with us?" For once, Oz's tone was actually friendly. But Katie crossed her arms and refused to budge.

Friends beeped their jeep's horn behind us and yelled for me to hop in. I looked at Eden. "You want to meet up with me tomorrow night?"

She nodded, smiling into my eyes. "How about six-thirty?" she asked. "There's a movie I've wanted to see."

"Sure," I answered. When we hugged, warmth pulsated through my body.

I was in for a surprise the next morning.

"We meet again," Eden said, taking the seat beside me. We were riding the shuttle, which took students back and forth from classes to the dorms and parking lots. Eden was headed to class while I was riding up the hill to my apartment in Drescher, the graduate apartments. I was reading Thoreau, but set him down, certain he wouldn't mind.

"So, I hear you're from Tennessee?" she asked.

"Yep, born and raised. And I have the cowboy boots to prove it."

Eden leaned her head back and laughed. Her presence was soothing, and she left me longing for more of it.

"And you're from . . ." I hinted.

"Colorado Springs."

"Yeah?" I said. "I hear it's beautiful there."

"It is. So what year are you?"

"I'm a graduate student in literature."

"Nice. I almost studied that."

"Really? What are you studying now?"

"It was nursing. But now, it's art history. I'm a senior." The shuttle slowed as it approached the next stop. Eden shifted her books in her lap and adjusted her purse on her shoulder. "Well, this is my stop."

"Wait," I said, leaning forward. I almost took her arm in my hand, but I hesitated. "We're still on for tonight?"

"Sure. They're showing *Invisible Children* tonight in Elkins at seven." *Invisible Children* is a documentary on child soldiering in Uganda.

"Okay," I said. "How about we meet at the fountain in front of Elkins at six-thirty?"

"Sounds good." She smiled, and I went on to my apartment.

The sun set, casting its ripe orange glow along the azure-blue ocean's edge. Remembering Eden was from Colorado Springs, and all the class and sophistication the city portrays, I decided not to wear my usual white t-shirt, ripped jeans and cowboy boots. Instead, I chose some of the only nice clothes I owned: a long-sleeved, button-down, baby-blue dress shirt and khaki pants.

The only reason I purchased the outfit was because some girls had remarked that the shirt brought out the blue in my hazel eyes. One of them even said I looked handsome. So I wore it. And I slid on my blue Pepperdine lacrosse hat and brown leather loafers.

Elkins Auditorium, a lecture hall with cinema-style seating, would be packed that night for the movie. In front of Elkins stood a round, cement fountain where water shot up from its center. Park benches encircled the fountain, and from there, you could watch the crashing waves in the distance and the sunset along the mountain cliffs.

Eden wore a starched, white dress shirt tucked into jeans with black, high-heeled shoes.

"So, have you seen the movie before?" I asked when we hugged each other. She was already standing in line, keeping a spot open for me.

"Yeah, I saw it at their first screening a few months ago," she answered.

"And you're watching it again?"

"Why not?" she said, shrugging her shoulders. "Have you seen it?"

"I have."

Eden laughed. "Well, why do you want to watch it again?"

"I liked it." I held my hands up in defense. Eden laughed at me, and I tucked my hands into my hip pockets, laughing, but nervous.

Though I didn't date much, I always believed in avoiding movies on a first date. There's hardly time to talk and get to know each other. But

Invisible Children set the tone for the kind of relationship Eden and I would have, for we both wanted to do something to help the world.

Afterward, Eden drove us to my apartment so I wouldn't have to wait for the shuttle. I invited her in for some red wine I purchased in Italy. Eden parked her car along the curb and we made our way to my apartment. "So, I overheard that you studied abroad your sophomore year," I said.

"In Italy," she replied. "We traveled around Europe on the weekends. I spent a lot of my free time volunteering at the local orphanage. It was amazing and fulfilling, you know, working with kids who never had parents or whose parents had abandoned them. It taught me a lot. I could see myself doing that for the rest of my life."

I tilted my head. "You mean you would leave your family and friends and all that America has to offer, give it all up and spend the rest of your life working at an orphanage?" I watched her closely for her reaction.

She winced and I immediately regreted my words. I can be too blunt sometimes.

"Not my entire life," she said. "But, yeah. Have you heard of Frederick Buechner?"

"Yeah," I answered, surprised. "The writer."

"Right. He said our calling is where our passion and the world's deep hunger intersect."

"I know that quote."

"Well, that's what I want. I want to be passionate about something and pursue it and make a difference."

"Is that why you worked with orphans?"

"I guess so. Our professors in Florence encouraged us to volunteer some of our free time when we weren't in classes during the week. Other girls went with me. A Catholic soup kitchen fed the homeless every day, but I wanted to work with kids."

"A life like that, to live like that, there's never a lot of money in it," I said.

"I know. But I don't care about that. I'd rather live a life I enjoy and be fulfilled than make a lot of money. I learned that a long time ago. And you? Have you had much experience with kids? I know you've been to other countries, but I'm not sure what you did."

"I worked with street orphans in Mongolia last summer. And I spent some time in North Africa a few years back where I received survival training from an ex–Marine Corp officer. So that was cool."

"What was Mongolia like?"

"The people were really depressed. Their faces always looked downtrodden, you know, like the weight of the world was on their shoulders. They came out of Soviet Communism back in the late eighties, and the girls went to the university while a lot of the men turned to vodka. Western men were beaten up during my time there, because

45

they were dating all the Mongolian girls. You know, I mean, what educated Mongolian girl wants to be with a drunken guy with no ambition or goals? So these Western men, owners and managers of drilling companies, coal and diamonds, they came in and all the pretty Mongolian girls flocked to them. So that didn't set well with the Mongolian men.

"One time, at a pub in the capital, Ulaanbaatar, this American guy from the Peace Corps had drinks with three Mongolian girls. He got jumped by six guys outside and was flown to China to have reconstructive surgery done on his face. You would think since Buddhism is so prevalent there, the people would have a more peaceful way about them. But it's not true."

"Hmm." Eden held my eyes, listening. "How did you end up there?"

"Well, I worked with a street kids' mission in Africa a few years ago and saw a newsreel on the internet from the BBC about a need for help with street kids in Mongolia. I contacted a non-profit there and sent them my résumé and asked if I could come and volunteer. They said yes, so I raised the funds through letters to non-profits and churches, and I went."

"How was it?"

"It was awesome. They didn't need me, though. The media made it look like there wasn't a lot of help. But there was. Four or five different organizations worked there. World Vision, Save the Children and a few others. I ended up volunteering at a summer camp with an orphanage."

Eden bit the side of her lip and smiled at me. I'm not sure how it happened, or when, but suddenly I realized she was standing only inches away from me. I leaned back and away from her, against the refrigerator. I had to lean away. Taking her into my arms would have been too tempting and too easy. And we barely knew each other. I was afraid contact like that might be too soon. Eden didn't strike me as someone who would rush toward physical affection until she really grew to know someone.

Feelings can erupt quickly and scare us. Yet, they thrill and dare us to grab on, tightly. It's an edge where life and death seem separated by a thin line. We know that if we love and live, then we can walk, run and fly. But if we love and lose, we fall and wonder if even crawling will ever be possible again.

When Eden yawned at three o'clock in the morning, I walked her to her car. "Why did you want to hang out with me?" she asked.

I pushed my hands into my pockets and tried to act cool. "Well, I can tell you what I think you want to hear or I can tell you the truth."

She exhaled through her nose with a short laugh. "Why wouldn't you tell the truth?"

I shrugged my shoulders. "Some people don't like the truth. If you ask me a question, I'll be honest with you."

Seconds passed.

"Well," she said, breaking the silence. "Are you going to tell me?"

"You want to know?"

Eden nodded, and that's when we reached her car.

I stopped and faced her. "Because I think you're beautiful. I know you're a good woman, and after listening to you tonight, I believe it all the more."

"I think you're a handsome and good-hearted person, too."

"You want to hang out again?"

"Yeah."

"I'll call you tomorrow." I opened the door for her. Eden stood still for a moment, looking over my shoulder, avoiding my eyes. She didn't want to leave, nor did I. When she returned her gaze to mine, she hugged me and then sat down in her driver's seat. I returned a fond smile and closed her door.

I don't remember walking back into my apartment that night. I was too busy trying to convince myself I felt nothing for her and that this night was just like any other night. I had hung out with a few attractive girls during my high school and undergraduate years. I never formally dated them, but I learned this: Girls are just people. And people will often say what they feel in the moment. Because of this, I had refused to allow myself to be vulnerable to any woman who I knew did not care deeply for me. "Pay attention to people's actions," Grandpa had instructed. "Not their words."

I didn't think there was a single woman in the world I wanted to be with, and I had no immediate plans to change that. But Eden had reached me in a way that I didn't think was possible. So, I fell asleep that night, without allowing my thoughts to dwell on her. But that was my last night maintaining that discipline.

The next afternoon, I was studying in Malibu, at Dietrich's, a quaint little coffee shop next to Malibu Yogurt and Ralph's Grocery. (Dietrich's burned down some years later, and a Starbucks was built in its stead.) Movie stars popped in from time to time. Pamela Anderson came in once, dressed in white. White jeans. White shirt. White shoes. Malibu isn't a big city. It's a beach town near Los Angeles, where city folk can take a day trip. Everything in Malibu closes at ten o'clock, to keep trouble out, I guess.

While at Dietrich's, I thought about Eden. I lifted my phone and sent her a text message, asking how her morning faired. She replied that she had finished studying and could meet me for coffee. Fifteen minutes later, she stood at my table.

"Hello," I said, glad to hear that I sounded collected.

"Hi."

"I've been studying a good while. You want to go to the beach?"

"Sure." We walked to her car and I opened her door for her. When we pulled out onto the Pacific Coast Highway, she turned on her radio and Coldplay's album *X&Y* blared through the speakers. She turned down the volume, laughing in embarrassment.

"You like Coldplay a lot, huh?" I said, teasing her.

"Yeah. It's great chill music. You want to ride with the windows down?"

"Sure." The wind whipped through the car as we talked over the music.

"Which beach do you want to go to?"

"Zuma, on down the road. Ryan and I go to a Starbucks there after hanging out at the beach."

"How far is Zuma?"

"It's a ways. Where were you thinking?"

"Westward Beach."

"I haven't heard of that one."

"Only the locals know about it."

"Sounds good to me."

We drove off PCH and onto a side paved road, which weaved through the hills for a few hundred yards until we came to the beach. The sun's warmth mixed with the scents of the sea. We parked on the side of the road and walked to the bank, where the sand lay compacted due to recent tides. Side by side, we walked and talked until the sun set.

Our only company was a few locals. An occasional seagull would glide near us, hoping to be fed.

"So, do you have any siblings?" she asked.

"Yeah. My brother, Caleb. He's a few years older than me."

"Do you two get along?"

"He's one of my best friends. We were roommates in undergrad. What about you? Any brothers or sisters?"

"I have a younger sister named Cynthia. She's sixteen. She's boy crazy," Eden said, laughing.

"Do you get along with her?"

"Yes. We're really close."

"Cool," I said. "So you told me you were studying nursing, but now it's art history. Why did you change?"

"My true passion is art. That's all."

"I don't know much about art history. You study the artists and the culture they came from, and what influenced their art?"

"Right," she said, sounding surprised. "That's part of it. How did you know that?"

"That's part of literature too, studying the culture of the writers, when and where they wrote the text. Do you have a favorite artist?"

"Caravaggio. He was from Italy. He painted

pictures of Biblical stories. In a lot of them he painted his own face on some of the characters. He grew up as a devout Catholic but when he was young, he killed a man in a drunken tavern fight."

"Wow."

"He fled and lived the rest of his life as a vagabond and painter."

"What are some of his paintings?"

"Well, there's the famous David and Goliath painting he did when he was a lot older. David's holding Goliath's head. David's face is young Caravaggio's, and Goliath's face is Caravaggio when he's older."

"The old man ashamed of the boy he was?"

Eden nodded. "And there's one where Abraham is about to sacrifice Isaac. Abraham has Isaac pinned to the altar and the angel is stopping Abraham. Caravaggio's face is believed to be painted as Isaac's."

"Do you know much about Rembrandt? His dark colors and browns and reds, they're really amazing."

"They are!" She clapped her hands and laughed. "I could go on for hours about all of this! I'm glad I have someone to listen."

"Hey, I'm all about it. I find that stuff fascinating."

"Really?"

"Sure. To find out where the creators came from and what happened in their lives that influenced what they created. You can tell a lot about art when you hear about the artist. When you hear their story, the art makes more sense. You discover what your instincts were right about but you learn things you never expected, too. It's interesting."

"I know. I love it. Rembrandt was a playboy."

"He was?"

"Yeah. When he was a young man, he wooed 'loose women,' but then in his sage years, he mourned the decisions of his past. Sometime I should show you the self-portraits he did of himself when he was a kid, compared to the ones he painted when he was an old man. Besides the wrinkles and age changes, they're very different."

"How?"

"Well, the earlier one is him as a young man, clean and fat with a healthy face and cheeks. He's leaning back and laughing at the artist. But in his older one, he just seems . . . so . . . I don't know. Sad. Regretful."

"The way you talk," I said. We stopped and looked at each other. "I've never heard a girl talk like you."

"My accent?"

"No. Just, your way with words. It's like reading something. You'd be a good teacher."

"Well, maybe I will one day."

"What are you doing after graduation?"

"I plan to go back to Colorado and work for my dad for a while. Save some money and try to get into Sotheby's in London. It's an art institute. It's one of the best in the world."

"I believe you can do it."

"You do?"

"Sure. Your grades are good here, right?"

"Three point five," she said, and I could tell she hoped that was impressive. "And you? What are your plans?"

"Apply for my Ph.D. at Vanderbilt, in Nashville."

"One of my best friends lives there! I love that place."

"My grandpa taught school there as a professor. It's a long story, but I'll tell you sometime. I want to hear more about you. Tell me something else."

"Like what?"

"Did you play any sports in school?"

"Volleyball. I was All-State in tennis."

"You didn't want to play in college?"

"No. It was fun but I wanted to do other things."

"Okay. Anything else?"

"I was a cheerleader. Is that bad?"

"No, because I know you probably didn't get wrapped up in the popularity chase."

"No, I didn't. I did it because I enjoyed it." She tilted her shoulders and maneuvered until the joints popped in her back. "But I was a thrower and wore heavy backpacks, so I know I'll have back problems later."

"I'm sorry."

"It's okay. What about you? Any sports?"

"I played basketball in high school. I still play pick-up games here in the gym at night. So that's fun. But I took it seriously in high school. My brother Caleb was better than I was. He won All-County and All-Tournament at different events. All I ever won was a trophy or two."

"That's good," she said, trying to encourage me.

"Well," I laughed, "everyone got trophies. They were like certificates of participation."

"Were you on the starting team?"

"Yeah, I started."

"See!" she said, poking my ribs. "You were good. What position?"

"Point guard."

"So you were the coach on the floor?"

"And you remember that from your cheer-leading years?"

Eden leaned her head back and laughed, sensing the playfulness in my tone.

"See!" I said, nudging her waist. "You would be a good teacher!"

"Well, eventually I want to be a curator. They work in museums and auction off paintings."

"Do you miss Italy?"

Eden blinked softly, looking over my shoulder, and I could tell she was remembering fond times. "Yes. I miss its beauty. I miss working at the orphanage. The children taught me a lot, more than I taught them."

"Like what?"

"Well, they taught me that sometimes all they need is to be held, to hug. There are so many of them and few nurses working there. The kids don't hug each other a lot, and so, sometimes, we just hugged them, played with them and let them sit in our laps. That meant more to them than feeding and teaching them."

I put my arm around her, pulled her close to me and kissed the top of her head.

"What was that for?" she asked, smiling.

"You're a good person."

"You are, too," she said, looking up at me. "You're the one who's traveled the world."

"Well, you have, too."

"Yeah, but on the weekends in Italy. You're the missionary. Do you think you'll ever do that full-time?"

"I'd like to, eventually. Maybe part-time. I want to do other things too, you know. Like get my Ph.D., teach, travel some more and study at Oxford one day."

"Oxford?" Her eyes brightened. "I want to study there too!"

"Really?"

"Yes! It's been my dream for a long time." Then she wrapped her arm around my waist, and we continued walking.

"Well, maybe you will one day. I've even thought about joining the military. Becoming a chaplain. I've always been fascinated with self-defense, underwater missions, building fires without matches and extracting water from tree leaves. You know, all the cool stuff you should learn in school but they only teach you in Boy Scouts."

"Were you a Boy Scout?"

"No, I'm just saying. I want the discipline, the knowledge in how to protect myself and my family in case something happens. And then there's the adventure part."

Eden had stopped walking suddenly and her whole body stiffened.

"What's wrong?" I asked her.

"Nothing," she said, but now she seemed miles away and looked upset.

I stopped and kissed her forehead. She leaned her head on my shoulder and lifted her chin. Our eyes met again. Silence. I don't remember the seagulls or where the people went. Her scent engulfed me. The wind pushed her hair against her face, and I took her cheeks into my hands and kissed her lips. I wrapped my arms around her, and finally felt her relaxing and returning emotionally to me. We spent the rest of the afternoon just like that, in silence, holding each other, and watching the waves crash, with the sunset as a backdrop.

Years have passed since that day at the beach, but I remember it as if it happened last week. I can still feel the sun's warmth on my skin. I can feel her hands on my waist. I can still see her eyes, gazing into mine. I can feel the ocean breeze, the wind lifting my hair, and I can still hear her laughter.

At that time, we would have both confessed that we were caught up in something much larger than ourselves. I knew, that day, that I wouldn't tell people about us, and I asked her to do the same.

"Okay," she answered, wincing.

"It's just that Pepperdine has enough to talk about." I knew she didn't understand, but I hoped she trusted me. I would have handled that differently if I had it to do over again. But I was young and afraid of losing her.

When we're young, we often let our friends do our thinking for us, rather than seeking counsel from an older mentor. During my undergraduate years, I witnessed couples (who genuinely loved each other) be torn apart by jealous or over-protective friends. In my mind, the less involvement youthful friends had within my relationships, the better. I didn't want my friends prodding or Eden's friends whispering unfounded rumors about me into her ears. I didn't want anyone to ruin it.

My friends would never understand how my feelings for Eden were developing so quickly. And I wasn't going to try explaining it to them. I had seen a lot of ugly in the world. And she was beauty. She was like a candle that soothes and comforts a child nervous in the dark.

"So what is this?" she asked, as we walked to her car, holding each other's hand.

"What do you want it to be?" I replied as I opened her door for her. Her hair fell over her shoulders and breasts. I raked my fingers through her dark strands.

She shrugged. "I think you're awesome."

"I think you're awesome, too. Why don't we just enjoy our time together, and we can let nature takes it course? When graduation comes, if we're still together, we can decide what we want to do. If not, we can be friends."

"Sounds good."

We drove back to campus and up the hill to Drescher graduate housing, where she dropped me off at my apartment. "Is there anything I can do for you before I go?" I asked, teasing her.

She shook her head and smiled.

"Do you have plans tomorrow night?"

"No."

"How about dinner? You name a place where we can get good Italian food, and I'll buy."

"How about Allegra's?" she asked.

"Okay."

The next night, we ate at Allegra's Italian on the Pacific Coast Highway. The aroma of fresh baked pasta, gourmet meats and spices rushed to my nose upon opening the door. Candlelight lit the tables, and the waiters wore white, starched shirts with black bow ties. The host placed us at a small, square table in a quiet corner by the window. After we sat, the voices of the people around us grew distant. Instead of sitting across from me, she sat beside me and I took her left hand and placed it on top of mine. And we sat like that, our hands embracing each other's, and talked the night away.

When the food arrived, I volunteered to say a prayer. After I said amen and looked back at her, I realized her gaze had never left mine. I liked the way she looked at me. I felt alive.

"So you mentioned you lived in North Africa and Mongolia for a while," she said, as she unfolded the napkin onto her lap. "Have you been anywhere else?"

"Backpacking or working?"

"Working."

"Yeah." I sat back in my chair and crossed one knee over the other. "I spent a summer teaching English in Romania. I traveled on the weekends. I saw most of the world during layovers or after the work was finished. You know, we'd have a layover in London or Rome, and instead of spending only a few hours, I'd have my travel agents make the layovers last two or three weeks. I got to see a lot doing that."

Eden leaned toward me, propped her elbows on the table, and rested her chin atop her hands. "You are so calm," she said.

"When you spend months traveling alone,

solitude happens," I said. "You deal with yourself. You think a lot. You think about the past, the present, the future. You put things to rest that bothered you for a long time. You contact old friends, or old enemies that were once friends, and you make it right, even if that means apologizing for things that weren't your fault. You deal with *you*. And there's another reason I'm calm."

"What?"

"You're here with me."

"Well," she answered, "I'm glad to be here."

"Me too."

Eden squeezed my hand, leaned in, and softly kissed my lips. When she drew her head back, I gently tugged her toward me. I kissed her bottom lip, pausing gently. When I let go, her eyes shone like the sun. From that moment on, our movements were like slow motion. Eden would bring her wine glass to her mouth, cut the pasta with her fork, every second lasting three; one second of life and then two more to reflect on the one that just occurred.

The food was sumptuous, adding a sensual mood to the evening. I had the waiter bring us two glasses of their house red. Therein, hints of chocolate and rich fruit left a thick spread across the glass. He presented an assortment of bruschetta before us, along with warm bread, fresh pressed olive oil, and salts. Fresh lasagna was ordered, every bite bursting with the ripe flavor of the tomatoes, as if they were just purchased from a local farmer's market; fresh San Marzano tomatoes, mashed into a creamy paste, between layers of soft pasta and blankets of Parmesan, ricotta, feta, mozzarella, and Pecorino Romano cheeses, all draped like a fine lace.

We also had green peppers, garlic, artichokes, and mushrooms, sauteed in Marsala wine, and roasted veal garnished with fresh basil, parsley, and ground black pepper with house vinegars and olive oil. A few more sips of that delicious red wine made everything seem right in the world. And after that, tiramisu.

When Eden stood and brought her chair next to mine, an elderly couple smiled at us. Eden leaned into my chest as I wrapped my arm around her. When I whispered into her ear, I found the words I chose were pronounced with eloquence and warmth. I had never spoken like that with anyone before.

We had made plans to watch a comedian on campus in Elkins at eight o'clock, but it was just seven when we arrived back on campus. So we went for a stroll in Alumni Park, a grassy lawn in front of Pepperdine that overlooks the coast. Deer wander down from the hills and rocky bluffs to graze there. The coral trees rise like watch-towers over a pond where freshwater reeds grow, providing a small refuge for ducks and wild birds. At night, a full moon leaves a trail on the ocean's black waters, and the constant coastal breeze disturbs the tree limbs, sending their leaves into a continuous stirring.

Eden and I stood beneath those trees, their limbs like liquid silver against the moon's glow. The waves crashed in the distance. She nestled her face into my neck and I wrapped my arms around her. We stood like that, silent for a while. The scent of her hair reminded me of the clusters of wildflowers that bloomed every summer in the pastures I played in as a child.

"Let's not go to the comedian show," she said, looking into my eyes and running her hands down to my hips.

"You want to go to my apartment so we can be alone?"

She nodded, so we hurried to my apartment and into my bedroom, away from all possible interruptions. I raised the blinds on my ocean-view window, and the full moon and the distant lights from Santa Monica sent a milky glow across my bedroom walls. I opened my laptop and turned on my favorite slow jazz. Every song was like something from a jazz club. Soft trumpets, a soft piano, a slow bass, a mellow voice.

We danced through five or six of the songs and spent the rest of the night staring out my window, holding each other. Sometimes, we lay together on my bed and took turns leaning over each other and talking. When she grew tired, she rested her head on my chest, occasionally whispering of her thoughts.

She told me about a boy she dated for four years. How they had been separated for five months when she met me. That she left him because he became verbally abusive.

When she asked me if I had ever dated anyone, I said no. I told her I was glad she was the only one. Eden glided her hands along my chest. Her fingers elicited feelings that had been buried and denied, feelings I believed never existed.

"Let's not get carried away," she said, when she knew things were growing hot between us.

"We won't."

Eden rested her elbow on my chest and propped her chin in her palm and looked down at me. I ran my fingers through her hair and tucked a few strands behind her ears. Her hair tie fell off and into my hand, which I slid onto my wrist.

"Your presence," I said, "is like water rushing over jagged rocks. Did you know that?" Eden hid her smile in her hand then leaned down and kissed me. I took her face in my hand, her velvety skin alive against my fingertips.

Her love for her family and for people who were hurting, along with her stunning beauty, made her irresistible. I kissed her forehead, her cheek, her neck and her chin. Our noses touched, and she drew a shaky breath. Her hair hung around my face, creating a veil that hid us from the world.

I could have stayed in that room with her forever. If she had shared with me all her insecurities, fears, mistakes and regrets, it could not have chased me away. She was like being home, and I was as much ease at with her as I was my own family.

I imagined my family meeting her. I knew they would love her, and if they didn't, I wouldn't care. Nothing or no one would deter me from being with her as long as she wanted me. I had never known romantic love. But whatever I was feeling and experiencing, I loved it.

"What are you thinking about?" She lay with her head on my chest, and I realized we had been quiet for a while.

"The winter's over," I said. I felt her smile against my shirt. I pulled out from under her, and she laid her head on my pillow. We kissed and paused at various intervals and continued those kisses until daybreak. Between midnight and three, she kept saying she needed to leave, but she remained in my arms. So, we whispered softly and kindly to each other for another two hours.

There were many times when she and I would look at each other, really look, and I found an untamable wildness in her eyes. She seemed to have the ability to accomplish anything she set her mind to. But something was holding her back from her dreams, as if invisible chains were wrapped around her ankles. And I promised myself that night, if I ever discovered what those chains were, I would help her break free from them. I would offer her myself, and I would say to her, "Come, take my hand, and I'll give you my word that anything you want, I will strive to provide for you if it's within my power. We'll explore this world together. We'll love and serve people, and never look back."

At five o'clock, as we walked to her car, we looked at each other and burst out laughing like children. "Is there anything I can do for you before you go?" I asked.

She shook her head and we parted, kissing, as the first beams from the sun burst forth behind us. When I returned to my bedroom, the scent of her hair remained on my pillow.

For the first time in my life, at the age of twenty-five, I was in love.

Chapter 2

The next morning, I reached for her, but she was gone. It all seemed too real. Too intense and too amazing. So much depth, everything I imagined romance between a man and woman should be. My growing admiration and respect for Eden was already surpassing all that novelists and poets attempt to describe. No painting or sculpture could portray it. "So this is what falling in love is like," I thought. Romantic love didn't disappoint.

I wanted to sing every song I had ever heard and every song yet to be composed. A fire of pure light burned in the depths of my heart, mind and soul, which could only be understood by seraphim. I wanted to live forever just so that such moments with her could be relived. I had met someone who made me want to say yes to anything she wanted.

As the days passed, Eden and I were inseparable. We spent every waking moment together. On Friday and Saturday nights, after every date and outing, I would walk her to her apartment door, and kiss her goodnight. On Sunday mornings, she would leave the sliding glass door to her bedroom unlocked. I would bring breakfast and fresh flowers for the vase on her dresser, wrap her in her blanket, and she would wrap her arms around my neck and hold on. Then I carried her onto her back porch, and we would watch the sunrise together.

We would return to Westward Beach and lie down on a blanket and watch the sailboats rocking their way to Marina del Rey. She would lay her head on my chest while I read the Victorian and Romantic poets to her: William Blake, John Keats, Shelley, Kipling, Robert Browning and Elizabeth Barrett.

"Read the one by Sheldon," she said once, as we lay under the coral trees in Alumni Park. I recited it from memory.

> "To hold her in my arms against the twilight and be her comrade for ever, this was all I wanted so long as my life should last. And this, I told myself with a kind of wonder, this was what love was: this consecration, this curious uplifting, this sudden inexplicable joy, and this intolerable pain."

Other students were scattered throughout the park, studying, talking, and throwing frisbees. I raked my fingers through her hair. "His wife had cancer and he stuck with her through it all," I said. "Isn't that beautiful?" Eden set the book aside. Hovering over me, she kissed me. I removed the hair tie from her hair, letting her dark strands fall into and around my face. Vanilla scents emanated from her hair. I wrapped the hair tie around my wrist while we kissed.

Under a distant shade tree, on a blanket, Oz, Katie, and classmates studied with drinks and snacks. Oz told me the story later. Apparently, Katie was watching us, with envy.

"How's your sense of entitlement?" Oz had asked her.

"What's your problem?" Katie snapped.

"You're everyone's problem," Oz answered. "You sorority girls and frat boys, when you don't get what you want, you take. Because you're spoiled. No one likes you."

Katie threw her iced coffee on him and stormed off. Oz just laughed. But this one frat boy, a foot taller and stronger than Oz, who had a crush on Katie, stood up to Oz. So Oz took a quick step toward him. "Do it!" he screamed.

All the guys in the study group shot from their seats and got between them, standing in front of Oz, holding him back. Oz would have torn him up. Oz was not a bad guy, for the most part, and a loyal friend. But he also had a temper, especially when it came to the Greeks.

At the time, all I heard was Oz scream, "Do it!" and saw him in the boy's face.

So I yelled, "Oz! Knock it off!" Because I was afraid he'd get into a fight, get sent before the administration, and they would discover he wasn't Irish. The frat boy chased after Katie and the conflict was over.

"What's up with him?" Eden asked.

"Oh, it's just Oz," I replied.

"I was going to tell you. I applied to Sotheby's," she said.

"In London?"

"Yeah."

"You'll get accepted."

"Will you come see me?" she asked.

"Of course. Maybe I can apply to school there too."

"In London? Really?"

"Yeah. And during school breaks, we'll travel the world."

The sun warmed our faces, and the breeze blew away its heat. Seagulls cackled back and forth to each other, and in the distance, we heard the waves crash and rattle against the banks. Life around us turned surreal, like watching yourself in a dream. Hummingbirds chased and fussed at each other. The tree limbs shook against the soft coastal breeze, and the bees browsed amongst the coral trees.

"What are you thinking about?" she asked.

"I love it here."

Eden's phone rang. Katie's name appeared on her caller ID.

"Hi, Katie," Eden answered.

I didn't appreciate Eden answering her phone

during our time together, as selfish as that sounds. And I certainly didn't like the caller being Katie. Hadn't she seen Eden and I together? Of course she had. Which is why she called. Doing all she could to interrupt. To come between us.

"Oh, just hanging out with Finn," she said.

I stood, annoyed, and Eden motioned me to wait. "Tonight? I'm not sure. I'll have to ask him . . . Yeah." Eden laughed and I stared off into the ocean, fuming. "Tomorrow? I have an exam . . . Mm hm . . . Let me call you late— I don't know what we're doing then . . . Okay. I'll . . . Okay. I'll call you later . . . I will. Bye."

Eden ended the call and hung her head. "I'm sorry," she said.

"Don't let Katie tell you what to do," I said, sharper than I intended.

"I don't. I—"

"What we do is none of her business."

"You've got her all wrong."

"I've seen the way Katie works a room," I answered. "She's—"

"She's what?" Eden said, standing.

"She's manipulative."

Eden crossed her arms and spoke with a tone I had never heard her use before. "You're not jealous of my friends, are you?"

"No, it's just that—"

"What?"

Her phone rang. Katie, again. Eden silenced it.

"She'll get between us," I said.

"You don't have anything to worry about."

"College girls talk," I said.

"Finn," she replied, curtly.

"It's true. Your friends don't have to be responsible for your decisions. That's why it's always so easy for them to give advice. They don't have to live with the consequences."

"What are you talking about?"

"She'll whisper lies into your ear."

"I think you need to get control of yourself," she answered, gathering the blankets and book.

"Wait," I said, realizing this wasn't going as I intended.

"No," she said. "I'll talk to you tomorrow." And she left.

The rest of that day was the longest day I can remember. I constantly checked my phone for any missed calls or texts. Even during dinner with Ryan and Oz, which frustrated them. But nothing. The next day, I couldn't take the unspoken words anymore, so I went to her apartment and knocked on her door.

Eden answered and stepped outside. I remember the look on her face. Her eyes were calm and she looked glad to see me.

"I'm sorry," I said.

"Me too," she replied and hugged me, tightly.

"I'm just scared that someone will get between us." And I meant that with every fiber of my being. The truth is, I was afraid of Katie. She was unpredictable.

Eden's hands held the sides of my face and she kissed my lips. "They won't," she whispered. "I promise." We held each other, pausing at intervals, kissing. "On our first date, you asked what I did when I wanted to be alone?"

"Yeah."

"I want to show you something," she said.

Eden led me to a back room in her apartment where sheets with paint smudges protected the walls and floor. The air was filled with sweet scents of fresh paint. A canvas on a tripod, two stools, and a paint set stood at the center of the room. Paintings, reflecting an influence of the Baroque period, hung on the walls: Eden's parents, her red retriever back home, and a portrait of Joanna. "You painted these?" I asked, turning back to her. But she was gone.

She re-entered wearing an old, light purple t-shirt, which intensified her brown eyes. Different swipes of paint covered her shirt. She wore navy shorts from her years in volleyball. The curves in her calves and quads sent a quick pulse up my neck and heat into my face. I looked away and swallowed hard, refusing to let my thoughts dwell there.

"I painted them," she said.

"I'm impressed."

She patted the stool, inviting me to sit. When I

agreed, she skipped to her canvas, tied her hair back and she painted my portrait over the course of about an hour.

"I think I'm done," she said. I looked at the painting, and was so moved by her secret talent, I really didn't know what to say. I just stared at her. "You wanna hear something funny?" she said. I nodded. "My parents and Joanna are the only ones who know I paint." She bit back a teary laugh and I took her cheeks in my hands and kissed her. She caught her breath and pulled back. "My birthday's this weekend."

"Happy Birthday!" I said, laughing.

"Thanks. But there's more. Back around Christmas, my parents ordered two tickets for me and a friend to fly to Colorado for the day. Birthdays are a big deal in our family. We've never missed each other's birthdays. My birthday's fallen on a weekday ever since I've been in college. Except this year. I want you to go to Colorado with me."

"Meet your parents this weekend?" I asked, surprised.

Eden searched my eyes. "Yeah . . . But you don't have to go if you don't want to."

"No, I do," I said, correcting my response. "I just . . . I didn't see that coming. I'd be glad to meet your parents." Eden smiled and kissed my cheek. Then she laid her head back down on my shoulder. "So when do we leave?" I asked.

"Saturday at noon. And it's a three-hour flight. So we'll arrive there at three o'clock. My sister, Cynthia, will pick us up at the airport. We'll have dinner and birthday cake at our home and then our flight back's at eight. Oh, and carry a jacket, because it's Colorado." I chuckled. "What?" she asked.

"It's sudden, but it'll be fun. I'm looking forward to it."

"Me too."

The night was late, she had some work to turn in the next day, and I needed to finish writing a paper. She walked me to her door. "So," she said. "Saturday it is."

"Yeah. Let's go down to Dietrich's on Saturday before our flight."

"Okay."

"Is there anything I can do for you before I go?" I asked.

"No," she said. I leaned down and we kissed each other's lips, held for a moment, and then followed with a peck goodnight.

"Finn, Valentine's Day is tomorrow."

"I know," I answered, smiling. Eden tried to bite back the grin that broke across her face, but she failed. "I have class until ten o'clock at night," I added. "But we can meet at my apartment and have some wine."

"Sounds good," she said, grinning. We kissed goodnight.

• • •

On Saturday morning, when I returned to my bedroom after my morning workout, I had a missed call from Eden. I returned her call and left a voicemail. "Hey, leave me a message next time. Your voice is soothing."

"My voice is soothing?" she said, brightly, when she called me later.

"Yeah."

"Are you on campus now?" she asked.

"Not yet. I'm about to take a shower and then come down. Do you want to meet me in an hour?"

She agreed, and we met at the fountain in front of Elkins. We greeted each other with a warm smile and hug and briefly sat at one of the cement tables.

"You packed?" she asked.

"Yep, and you?"

"I am, and I'm glad you're coming with me."

"Well, I'm honored by the invitation."

After we loaded our luggage in the car, we journeyed into Malibu and found a parking place in Malibu Colony, where the cafés and stores still stand today. There, townspeople and students eat yogurt near the fountain, while children play in the water. Maroon sun umbrellas provide shade over the café tables, and the fountain's heavy water pounds, sending an echo across the street. Wild birds chirped from the trees, and street

76

pigeons scouted beneath tables for crumbs as Eden chose a seat for us outside, and I entered Dietrich's to order our drinks. Aromas of fresh brewed coffee, scorched chocolate, and fresh breads spilled onto the sidewalks.

I purchased two mint teas, and then I heard Oz in the corner, speaking in his Irish accent. He was entertaining some Malibu girls on the sofa. He saw me and sprang from his seat.

"Finn!" he exclaimed, then looked back at the lovely girls and set his hot tea on the table. "Excuse me, girls. That's my pal over there."

I wasn't sure if the girls were college freshmen or high school seniors. The girls from Malibu High were known to look older. Oz wasn't a Casanova, but he wasn't the hunchback of Notre Dame either. He exercised regularly and drank fresh fruit juices. He proudly sported a shaved head and wore trendy jeans, sneakers, and aviator-style sunglasses even when it wasn't sunny. He had good street smarts, and knew how to be serious and light-hearted at the right times.

"Hey, Finn," he said, shaking my hand and throwing his other arm around me.

"Ya keepin' the girls entertained, lad?" I said, mocking his fake accent.

"Ah, Finn, ya know me. I can't get enough of the SoCal girls."

"They're not sorority girls, are they Oz?"

"Of course not," he smirked. "So how's it going

with that girl?" he said, bringing his voice down to a whisper.

"Ah," I said, shrugging it off. "It's cool. Just seeing how it plays out."

"Oh, just to give you the heads-up. When you and Eden were out here the other day, Katie was watching you two. Watch out for her. She's trouble."

"Yeah. I'm aware. Thanks though."

"Okay, Finn," Oz said, raising his voice as he backed away. "I gotta return to the girls. Wouldn't want them to get cold over there." Then he flopped back down onto the sofa. Both girls were blondes, but with brown roots. They wore v-neck t-shirts, push-up bras, and tiny shorts that could be mistaken for underwear. One of the girls was biting her straw and smiling at Oz. One tanned knee was crossed over the other. The other Malibu girl sat at the edge of her seat and liked to throw her chin up when she laughed. They hung onto Oz's every word in his thick, Irish accent.

"That's me pal, Finn. Good lad, good lad," I heard him say. But the girls never looked in my direction.

When Oz first arrived at Pepperdine, I found him sleeping in the library at two o'clock in the morning. Pepperdine's library is open twenty-four-seven, and Oz would sleep on a mat in the library and take his showers in the locker room in the gym. He kept his suitcases and clothes in a friend's closet in one of the dorms. In the library, Oz found an aisle in the collection of dictionaries on the third floor, because no students ever traveled there, especially not after eleven at night. The dictionaries, being next to the history section, led me straight to him.

One night when I couldn't sleep, I walked down to the library to look for a book on Jonathan Edwards and the establishment of Princeton. Browsing through the history section, I spotted Oz's mat and blankets through the metal book-shelves. I woke him and invited him to stay with Ryan and me, since we had a spare room in our apartment.

Over time, Oz became friends with us and established trust. He confessed who he was one morning over breakfast. Though Ryan and I never chided him for his lies, the lies weighed on him, heavily. When the three of us were in public, and Oz had to be Irish, he couldn't look at me and Ryan. I guess he felt ashamed.

It wasn't long after that we were cooking dinner one night and he asked me what I thought would happen if he confessed to Pepperdine who he really was. I told him I didn't know. But I said, "I do look forward to the day when you decide to make it right. We'll be there for you, whatever Pepperdine decides to do."

I could write an entire tale about Oz and his adventures. But this one belongs to Eden.

• • •

I mixed milk and honey into our tea and walked out the door to our table. I hung my coat around Eden's shoulders because the sky was overcast, and the air was chilly. I sat down, and we talked until it was time to leave for the airport. "So," she said, sitting in her chair facing me, cupping her tea in her hands. "Colorado."

"Yeah," I answered, smiling.

"Why does everyone call you Finn? They just decided to shorten your last name?"

"Not exactly," I said with a laugh. "There's this creek behind my grandpa's house back home. It branches out into a cascade of waterfalls, some of them fifty feet high, and it empties into a pool we call the blue hole. My brother Caleb and my cousins and I used to go fishing and swimming there. Once while we were fishing, I had this expensive lure. Granted, it was only five dollars, but that's a lot of money for an eight-year-old. That lure caught some of the biggest bass you'd ever see. It worked better than chicken livers.

"So this brim—a small fish, too small to cook—grabbed my lure and hook. I reeled him in, gripped his slippery body, and just as I tried to pull out the lure, the brim finned me, slicing the web between my thumb and forefinger. I dropped the fish, and it wiggled its way back into the water. I had my hook, but the brim had swallowed the lure. I shouted every curse word imaginable.

Caleb and my cousins thought it was hysterical. So since I got 'finned,' that's how I got the name. Caleb started it, my cousins and friends caught on, and eventually even my parents and Grandpa started calling me Finn. But when my family needs to talk to me about something serious, they always call me Clayton."

Eden was raised in a large city, and found stories of small-town life fresh and charming.

"It was a good life," I said. "My mom stayed home and raised us while Dad and Grandpa worked."

"I want to stay home when I have children too," she said.

"Oh, I agree. Mom stayed at home until we were in junior high. Then she went on to teach middle school math. I wouldn't have it any other way."

"I told my dad about you," she said.

"You did?"

Eden nodded with a smile, tightening her lips.

"What did he say?" I asked.

"He said, 'Finn? As in Huck Finn?' "

We both laughed while trying to swallow our tea. The moment softened, and we looked at each other in the quiet. "I can't get enough of you," she said.

Warmth passed through my body as if someone had doused me with a pail of warm water after I had been treading through the snow. How can words from another human make someone feel so alive?

Some kids splashed water at each other in the fountain, and a puppy darted under our feet, dragging its leash and chasing a loose ball.

"Your parents," I said. "What are they like?"

"I love them very much," she answered. "My mother visited me during my sophomore year and met all my sorority sisters. After she got home, she wrote each of them a letter of encouragement, saying kind, sweet things, letting them know she cared about them and was praying for them. Some of the girls came to me later with tears in their eyes because the letters meant so much to them. Even Dad writes me letters. When I'm home, he takes me out on dates. When I need advice and stuff like that, he's usually the one I call. He just always knows what to do."

"Sounds like a good dad."

"He is. Tell me," she said. "What are your parents like?"

"My mother is very lovely. A kind spirit," I answered. "Polite, humble and very beautiful. She always made breakfast for Caleb and me when we were young, and she worked in the flower beds at the side of our house. In the spring, she picked buttercups every morning and placed them in a vase on the dining room table. She always listened patiently to everything Caleb and I said. She was always interested in our lives, no matter how frivolous our stories were.

"She went to college while Caleb and I were in

elementary school. And she still managed to cook breakfast and dinner for us. All farm food, made from scratch stuff, you know. And Dad, he was our basketball coach when we were in elementary school. Now, he's in the cattle business. He's a good dad.

"My grandpa also helped raise us. He's the wisest man I know. He was a paper boy growing up and read the papers every morning before he delivered them to people's homes. Eventually he began writing for the newspaper and was later hired on as an editor at a publishing company. He took college classes in the evening and worked during the day. Later he began his own newspaper company. Because of his reputation in town, he was invited to give guest lectures at Vanderbilt and Lipscomb Universities on journalism and ethics."

"What a great story."

"Grandpa even spent a summer in Africa doing volunteer medical missions when he was my age."

"And you've been to foreign countries yourself. Do you think you'll ever go back?"

"I'd like to. What I'd really like to do is go to Paris and study French. Two foreign languages are required for my Ph.D."

"For your Ph.D. in literature?"

"Yeah."

Eden tapped my knee with her hand. "Take me with you!"

"I can if you want. But you'll have to stick around for a while," I said, playfully.

She laughed and pulled her knees to her chest and hugged them. I watched her, drinking in the sight of her. "So our dinner's tonight. Are you dressing up?" she asked.

"I'm planning to wear black slacks and a button-down dress shirt."

"I'll dress up for you."

"You don't have to dress up for me. You can come in a t-shirt and sweatpants for all I care." Her smile faded. "Hey," I added, regretting my words. "If you want to dress up for me, I'd love that."

Her smile broke free across her face. "Okay!"

I really didn't care if she dressed up or not. I just wanted to be in her presence. I think she understood that. I remember an image of her that day. Her back was to the fountain. She was wrapped in my jacket, almost swallowed by it. You never realize how small a woman is until she wears your clothes. She sipped her tea with her mug cupped in both of her hands, blowing away the steam. Our eyes met and she smiled, and I remember thinking that she was amazing.

We went to the airport and took our seats on the plane. She asked if she could sit beside the window, and I let her. We buckled in, and she grabbed my arm with her hands and smiled at me.

"So," I began. "Give me the scoop. What's Colorado Springs like?"

"Mmmm," she said, grinning. "Well, every fall, there's a hot-air balloon festival. Hundreds of balloons are scattered in tiers across the sky. They shoot up at sunrise and you can hear all the flames blasting. They fly over Memorial Lake and the balloons reflect off the water. When the aspens are in full bloom, you know, the different colors of leaves, it's beautiful. We're known for outdoorsy stuff like mountain biking and rock climbing."

"Do you snowboard?"

Eden laughed under her breath and shook her head. "No," she said, embarrassed. "I had a terrible experience as a kid on the slopes, and I never went back."

"Really? What happened?"

"Nope." Eden shook her head. "I'm not telling you."

"Well, maybe one day you will. So, what else?"

"Mmmm," Eden hummed, tapping her chin with her forefinger, making me starve for more. "Let's see. Well, I went to Colorado Springs Christian High School. It's relatively small, about five hundred. We're the largest Christian school in Colorado Springs, maybe in all of Colorado. Really good college recruitment, you know, lots of students go on to major universities. Every Christmas, my family and I go to the symphony. Our philharmonic is world renowned. When I was a little girl, we always went to Michelle's for ice cream after the orchestra."

"Michelle's?"

"It's an ice cream parlor on Tejon Street downtown. It's been there for over one hundred years, the oldest business in the city. Even the signs are made from the kind of light bulbs that were popular before neon lights."

"Wow."

"Yeah, right. With those old-fashioned signs and that old-fashioned feel, it's like you're in the 1950s when you walk in. Lots of high school kids go there on Friday and Saturday nights because Michelle's had this dish called 'The Flaming Mt. Olympus.' They brought it out on this huge, long plate, and it fed twenty people."

"One ice cream to feed twenty people?"

"Yep. Does your town have anything like that?"

"Kind of, but it's not as charming as yours. Well, maybe in a different way, I guess."

"Tell me."

"Well, I came from a much smaller town. Athletics is religion. When you live in a country town of barely over a thousand people, the neighboring towns average the same number. The nearest shopping mall is about an hour's drive away. I mean, you hop on the interstate and you drive an hour. It's that far."

"Wow."

I laughed. "I know. So sports, churches and

farms are the talk of the town. Small town politics is a big deal. When I was little, Caleb and I used to ride our bikes to Ol' Green's Store. It's a little shop a mile or so outside our hometown."

"Ol' Green's?"

"Yeah, Old Man Green, we used to call him."

Eden laughed, leaning her head back. I noticed how pretty her teeth were and how her eyes turned to squints when she laughed really hard.

"Old Man Green sold groceries, snacks, cokes, and tobacco. He dressed in overalls, and his wife always wore a flannel shirt. They tried to sell gasoline, but there were never enough cars passing through. They tied a bell to the front door of the store to let them know when customers came in. But it also warned them because kids would dart in and out with a handful of candy."

"I guess you were never that kid."

"No," I said, seriously. "But the scene, the atmosphere, it's all fond memories."

"Tell me more about your parents."

"Grandmother Fincannon died of a heart attack when Dad was eight, so Grandpa had to raise eight kids. Six girls and two boys. They were raised in the South, you know, so everyone, even the girls, have this tough side about them that they like to show off, even if they have to fake it. I remember once we were sitting at the dining room table over breakfast and Dad looked at me and Caleb and said, 'Boys, if I ever hear of you hitting a woman,

I'm coming after you. If you're gonna hit someone, you better hit someone who can fight back.' I remember because he was pointing a butter knife at us and strawberry jam was dangling on its end."

Eden chuckled. "Yeah, he taught you southern boys right," she said, poking my ribs.

"He never let us quit anything."

"No?"

"If we started a sport, he told us not to quit until the season was finished. That rule applied to everything. He'd say, 'Don't stop cutting the grass until it's done. Don't leave until the wood is stacked and the brush is piled. Stick out the season. If you don't want to go out for the team next year, that's fine. But don't quit. You quit now, and it'll be easier to quit later.' When Caleb and I fell off our bikes, he'd tell us to get up and try again. If I scraped my knee, he said to rise and shake off the dust. 'Get up, son. Get up,' he would say. 'You're not gonna get anywhere a'layin' down.' He taught us to hunt and fish, to say 'Sir' and 'Ma'am' and please and thank you. Dad coached our basketball teams in elementary school, and purchased jerseys, shoes, and trophies for kids who were too poor to afford them. Those kids were some of my best friends until high school."

"What happened?"

"Puberty, I guess. For some reason, at that age, we competed for everything."

"Mmmm," Eden said. "When we entered middle school, girls just got mean. Mean to each other."

"I don't know what causes it. Hormones, I guess."

"And your mom?"

"She's from Florida. Her grandparents lived in our hometown in Tennessee, so her dad wanted to move there. When he came home and shared the news, that they were moving back to Tennessee, she started crying because she didn't want to marry a hillbillie."

Eden burst into laughter, covering her mouth with her hand. People on the plane looked at us.

"Mom's a proper woman."

"She is?" Eden still giggled.

"Yeah, she wore dresses in public but dressed like a country girl at home. The earliest memory I have of her is her cut-off, blue-jean shorts, a white, v-neck t-shirt, and a red bandana in her hair, walking barefooted across the grass in our front yard. She made us wear shirts to the dinner table, made us give thanks for our food and pray before we went to bed. I may have told you earlier, but we had vegetable and flower gardens in our side-yard. Mom spent her afternoons there."

"My mom was like that too. She was a stay-at-home mom until we got older. She raised us to be ladies."

"Well, you are a lady."

"Thank you."

"What were you like as a kid?" I asked.

"Growing up as a city girl, I loved high school sports. I went swimming and mountain biking and stuff like that, but I really loved volleyball and tennis. And I hate to admit this because so many people get the wrong impression, but . . ."

"What?" I asked.

Eden paused for a moment, wondering if she should tell me. "I was a debutante."

"A debutante? You mean you went to a debutante ball?"

"Right, but there's more to it than that. You train for months and even go to a dinner training party when you're a freshman. And then you're 'presented' to society. It's fun, you know. I mean, people don't do that stuff anymore. Men don't 'present' their daughters for men in society to go after."

"It's tradition."

"You know, for ladies who like that kind of stuff. It's a very social thing to do."

"So what all do they teach you? How are you selected to be one?"

"Well, there's a woman in Colorado Springs. She has the right network. All the ladies in her social circle are former debutantes, or they had daughters who were debutantes. Or maybe they've contributed a lot to the tradition. They've married the right men in the right social circle, something like that."

"Like a rich ladies' society."

"Well, you don't have to be rich. It's other things, like having good grades, doing things in your community, or serving abroad. You know, like giving piano lessons for free to younger girls. For instance, we had this one girl spend one of her high school summers studying ecology in South America. Eighteen to twenty girls are selected during the winter of their senior year, and there's a party during the next summer, one party every three weeks."

"A party every three weeks? What do they do?"

"They're themed parties. Mother-daughter party, then a daughter-father party. There's a tea party and a garden party where they serve bananas foster and light it on fire. One time, we all came in poodle skirts, and there were gifts for us like perfume and stuff."

"So, do you let it be known that you want to be a debutante?"

"No, it's not like applying. You don't send in an application or photos or a résumé. You're just known. The girls are selected by all the other moms of past debutantes."

"And what do they teach you?"

"Well, in middle school, if you want to one day be a debutante, you go to Cotillion."

"Cotillion?"

"Yeah, it's just a name. It's from the Emily Post book of etiquette. From the 1920s. You learn how to throw a party, be a good hostess and properly serve tea, how to use silverware beginning from the outside and moving in, how to introduce a lady to a man and vice versa. You learn ballroom dancing, how to eat soup, pass food, place your glass on your right or left, how to set a banquet table and how to take and give a name card."

"A name card. You mean a card with your name on it?"

"Right. Kind of like a business card but it has your name on it."

"That's it? Just your name? You're right," I said, cocking a brow. "I mean, God forbid you'd have to write the person's name down on paper."

Eden clucked her tongue and popped my chest with the back of her hand. "Oh yeah," she said as she patted her knee. "We learn to curtsey. Putting one leg behind the other and bowing. But you have to do it while wearing a petticoat. They even have a mock debutante ball where you go through all the steps and you take your bow."

"What's a petticoat?"

Eden laughed. "You're just learning all kinds of stuff, huh?"

"Yeah, it's interesting."

Eden looked at me with a wry smile.

"What?" I asked.

"Okay," she continued. "Just wanted to make sure you're not teasing me."

"No, I want to know."

"Okay. It's when your gown goes out from your waist like an umbrella, and it has fluffy material underneath."

"And then eventually you have the debutante ball."

"Yep. They have it every year at the five-star Broadmoor Hotel. Famous people and former presidents stay there when they visit Colorado Springs. Every girl wears a white dress with gloves that go to the elbow. And these dresses can run up to three thousand dollars. Some girls buy dresses handed down from past debutantes. Other girls sit with their mothers and make their dress. My mom and my grandmother and I made my dress together. Grandmother came over every Tuesday and Thursday and we sewed and cut. It was really nice. I really enjoyed my time with them."

"That's sweet," I said, appreciative of her love for her family.

"It was sweet. Oh, and there were rules for the gown. It had to be pure white. It couldn't have any adornments or beads, the straps over the shoulder had to be a certain width and the circumference of the petticoat must be a certain size. You needed two male escorts, along with your dad. One or both of the escorts could be a brother, as long as he was sixteen. The escorts could be cousins or close friends, but not a boyfriend, because you might break up with him sometime later and now he's in all the pictures."

"Good idea," I said, laughing. "Sounds like the older ladies learned that from experience."

"Yeah. So these boys, they present her to society. The escorts wear tuxedos with tails and white gloves. They're like her protectors, signifying that they'll be there for her for the rest of her life. Then there's a father-daughter dance. When the time is right for her to be presented, her name is read along with her accomplishments, her education, and the volunteer work she's done. She curtsies and then she walks off the stage. Her parents and immediate family are introduced to everyone, and then the rest of the night is a party and a dance."

"Ballroom dancing?"

"Yeah, but they have some booty-music too," she answered, ending with a laugh.

"Well, that sounds like it was a lot of fun." I wished I could have been there to see it: to hear about the lessons she learned, to witness her recognized as a young woman, to meet her grandparents and to see a side of her life I was too late for.

"You talked about your grandfather," Eden said. "He sounds like an interesting guy. Did he do anything else besides publishing?"

"He lives across the road from us. At night, when Caleb and I were little, we took turns staying the night with him. We'd just walk across the road. He worked in the flower gardens that filled the front yard and bordered his house. Grandma had planted them before she died, and Grandpa kept them growing. I suppose it was one of his ways of keeping her alive. People often stopped by his house just to admire the roses, tiger lilies, annuals and perennials. His backyard's a green field, overrun with sage grass and yellow and purple wildflowers. Caleb and I used to play there growing up."

"My grandfather built our house for my grandmother when they were in their early twenties," Eden said. "He built it with his own hands. His family ran a small construction business that built homes and buildings for people in the community, so he had been around it all his life. Men volunteered to help him, but he wanted to do it himself. Mom and Dad renovated it and added an upstairs, but the rest of the house is as it was. I don't want you to get the wrong idea about my family. We're not snobby. Living in that area of Colorado Springs might seem like we have a lot of money, but we don't. I mean, some people might think we are rich compared to the rest of the world, I know, but we aren't rich like most of the people in our neighborhood."

"It sounds like your grandparents were amazing people. I wish I could have met them."

"Me too," she said, sandwiching my hand between hers. She reached and put her arm around me and pulled me to her, sliding her fingers through my hair, down my neck, and into my hair again.

Experiencing the touch from a woman you love brings comfort and ease. You see the beauty in all things that exist in the world, all your problems dissipate, and everything is suddenly okay. Nothing seems as bad as it once did. That's the power a good woman has over a man.

Chapter 3

When we arrived in Colorado Springs, Eden's sister, Cynthia, picked us up at the airport. She pulled over to the sidewalk outside baggage claim and leaped out of her car, laughing and bounding over to Eden, almost tackling her. A sharp gust of Colorado's February wind sent my hands into my pockets. "We've heard all about you, Finn!" Cynthia said, laughing. A bit shorter than Eden, she was dressed in a scarf with matching mittens, and her blonde hair was tied into a ponytail. Cynthia skipped to the driver's side, hopped into her seat. I opened the passenger door for Eden, and then I sat in the backseat.

"Is there a wine shop on the way home?" I asked. "I want to get some wine for the dinner."

"Sure," Cynthia said. "There's one on Tejon Street."

We drove out of the parking lot and found the freeway. Dark, green, rolling plains stretched to the east and looked mushy due to the recently melted snow. Snow-capped mountains, with white trenches cascading down their sides, stood in the distance. We entered downtown and passed by Colorado College. Freshly paved sidewalks met brick corners with flowerbeds in their centers. Hardwood trees grew an equal measure apart.

I wished I could see the town in autumn. Downtown's streets were clean, and the areas between all the buildings were grassy with places to sit for lunch. Very child-friendly. Above the buildings, the mountains were still visible, their snowy peaks a different shade of white against the overcast sky.

Cynthia pulled over to a curb and pointed toward the wine shop. "There it is."

"I'll be right back." I entered the store and told the ladies working behind the counter that I was visiting a family for dinner and we needed two bottles of wine, preferably two different vintages. The ladies picked out their two best sellers. I scooted out the door with two paper-sleeved bags.

Cynthia was talking a hundred miles an hour when I opened the car door. "All set?" she asked.

"Yep."

We drove about a mile into a suburb, took a couple of turns, and parked alongside a curb in front of a blue Victorian-styled home with white trim. Smoke rose from a chimney, and a wrap-around porch held a swing that swayed back and forth in the breeze.

At the front door, I reached out to ring the doorbell, but Eden slapped my hand. "Don't," she said, laughing at me. She swung the door open to aromas of fresh baked bread and roasted turkey.

"Hey! There they are!" Mr. Valmont exclaimed.

He wore reader's glasses, a collared shirt with a sweater over it, and had a head full of white hair. He stood aside, with a smile, inviting us in.

Every light in the house was on, and the threshold opened into a foyer of polished wood floors, with the living room and dining room in full view. Covered food and drinks garnished the dining room table, awaiting all the guests. Easy listening music played from speakers perched in the corners of the ceilings. French dining plates, glasses, and silverware reflected the light. The crackling and snapping of a fire came from another room.

My hands were full, so Mr. Valmont hugged me and then he hugged Eden. Mrs. Valmont, whose features favored Eden, sat in a wheelchair and rolled over to us. She hugged us both.

"We've heard a lot about you," Mrs. Valmont said. "Good things."

A red retriever named Boots jogged into the room, wagging his tail. Eden kneeled and rubbed his face and behind his ears. I bent down and petted him too, which was a mistake because he wouldn't leave me alone after that. He followed me around, pressing his head against my hand the entire night.

"Oh, you brought wine! Good!" Mrs. Valmont said.

"It was Finn's idea," Eden replied, wanting me to have the credit.

"Where did you get it?" she asked, pulling out one of the bottles and examining it. Mr. Valmont took the other bag and slid out the second bottle.

"The wine shop on Tejon," Eden added.

"Oh, that's where we buy our wine, too. Good choice, Finn," Mrs. Valmont said, smiling.

"Sure is," Mr. Valmont agreed. "Thank you."

"Well, the meal's prepared," said Mrs. Valmont, gesturing toward the dining room table. "But we'll wait on everyone else." The cherry-oak table had twelve cushioned, wooden chairs around it, five chairs on both sides of the table and a chair at both ends.

"We can sit in the living room until they arrive," Mr. Valmont said.

The living room was the center of a comfy, worn home of a family who'd raised multiple children. Large crème-colored couches and chairs were embroidered with maroon and white flowers on vines. The couch cushions were broken-in with blankets folded over the couch backs. Pillows were stuffed in the corners. Family photos and a large mirror sat on a fire mantle. I imagined Christmas stockings hanging there and a fully decorated Christmas tree in the corner.

Opposite sides of the room held end tables and chairs in the Victorian style, facing a piano. Lamps depicted paintings from the Romantic and Victorian eras; British and French men stood holding feathered hats at their hip with a knee propped on a stone and sitting women adorned in elaborate dresses with exposed shoulders and cleavage held fancy umbrellas.

The Valmonts were very educated, but not stiff. They seemed very . . . normal, if there is such a thing as normal.

Mr. Valmont poured us all a round of wine. Cynthia drank a glass too, but Mr. Valmont only filled it half full. We talked about everything, from the Malibu sunsets to the difficulties of our professors to the raccoons that raided the campus garbage cans at night. As we laughed and I heard stories of Eden's childhood, I would pause and just look at her. I saw a young woman loving her time with the people in her life she loved most. No poetry, literature, or song could ever express the depths of my thankfulness and gratitude for being there. Her family received me warmly, making sure I felt welcomed.

That experience made me think about my view of marriage. I always thought choosing a wife, a life-long companion, would be difficult. I used to wonder if it would ever be possible to look at a woman and know I loved her and wanted to spend the rest of my life with her. And then it happened. There I was. I knew loving Eden would be the easiest, most natural path.

I once sneered at comments like, "He fell in love," because Grandpa always taught love is action. I still believe that. But I now understood what people meant by the expression. You really are just living your everyday life, walking around, and then you trip. Just as you realize what's happening, you've already fallen. It's too late.

Eden's family asked about my parents and my home life. I told them everything I had already told Eden. "Mom stayed home and raised me and Caleb, while Dad went to work."

"That's what we wanted, too. And we did it," Mr. Valmont said.

"I raised them at home while he went to work," Mrs. Valmont added. "I couldn't bear to leave them with someone else."

"That's right," Mr. Valmont said. "I would come home for lunch and be able to see my wife and girls. Sure, we did without a lot of material things, but it was worth it. Love, family, it's worth it. When you can figure out what you need versus what you want, you're onto something."

"What about you two?" I asked. "How did you meet?"

Mr. and Mrs. Valmont looked at each other and grinned. When Mr. Valmont took her hand into his, her eyes radiated.

"After our first date, I told her I was going to marry her," Mr. Valmont said.

I laughed and asked Mrs. Valmont, "What did you say to that?"

She waved a dismissive hand. "I thought he was funny. But he believed it and he kept pursuing me."

"She was wonderful," Mr. Valmont said. "I didn't become a Christian until I was in college, and she had been raised in a Christian home. She had my respect and admiration. She had a very solid understanding of the world. She was very grounded. I had never met a woman quite like her. I was in awe. She was a year older than me, and I fell in love with her. I knew that first night. I just knew."

"And so you met in college?"

"Yes, my senior year," he answered. Boots licked my hand, and so I scratched his ears. He stood there, waiting until my hand grew tired. "She had already graduated, but our friends introduced us. Her parents lived in Colorado Springs, and so we came out here to be close to them. I got a job at a financial consultant company and eventually took over the business. So what about you, Finn? Where do you think you'll end up?"

"I don't know, exactly. It doesn't really matter that much to me anymore, because I've learned the only thing that has brought any fulfillment to my life is pouring myself out in service to others. I can do that wherever I am. I've always wanted to get my Ph.D. in literature and be a professor at Vanderbilt. My grandpa has been a huge influence in that area. I'd like to take college students to other countries during the summers so they can serve in humanitarian work. But I don't know where I'll end up. I once believed I could discern God's voice from my own heart. But experience has taught me that I only know God has spoken when I examine my life in hindsight."

"That's a good lesson to learn, Finn," Mrs. Valmont said.

"And you've traveled quite a bit, I understand," Mr. Valmont asked.

"Yes, sir. I've been to a few places."

"Eden told us about all the traveling and work you've done," Mrs. Valmont said. "That's really good, Finn." She looked me in the eye and smiled like a proud aunt. "And what have you learned from all those experiences?"

I looked down at the remaining wine in my glass. "That people are basically the same everywhere. If you pinch a kid in Germany, he'll say 'ouch.' If a man in Egypt loses his wife, he'll mourn. Right now, there are parents in Mexico discussing whether or not they should spank or ground their kids. Kids in Swaziland are arguing over a toy, saying things like, 'But I let you borrow mine yesterday.' I've learned that helping others is the only thing that's really given me a sense of meaning and purpose in life. The poverty and suffering I've seen, it makes me grateful for things I once took for granted, like having two eyes and two ears and two legs that work properly. I have good health, and I've never been hospitalized. I have a family who loves me. I think about things like that these days."

Mr. Valmont nodded his head, looking down at the coffee table and rubbing his wine glass between his thumb and forefinger.

"Very good, Finn," Mrs. Valmont said, looking over at her husband. "It sounds like you've learned a lot and that the Lord is with you."

"I hope He is."

"Oh, He is," she said, reassuring me. "He is."

Mr. Valmont passed behind his wife and whispered something into her ear that made her smile. Then he went to the kitchen and returned with a white cake with pink icing that read, *Happy 22.* Mrs. Valmont pulled a small, wrapped box from under the piano seat and brought it to Eden.

"We thought we'd do this before everyone arrived," she said.

Eden hugged her parents, whispered thank you, and blew out the candles. Then she opened the box to find a sterling-silver, heart-shaped charm to add to her bracelet. Her parents had purchased that bracelet for her when Eden graduated from high school and added a charm to it every year on her birthday.

Mr. Valmont cut out slivers of the cake for everyone. "We'll save the rest for after the dinner." Cynthia gave Eden an envelope with a handmade card. Inside the envelope was a gift card to their favorite coffee shop in town. *Hurry back* she'd scribbled. Eden hugged Cynthia and when she let go, Cynthia wiped tears out of her eyes.

Even though I hardly knew her family, and I know I'll never see them again, I miss them. I still think about them often. I wonder how Mr. Valmont's business is going and if Mrs. Valmont is still as happy as she seemed that evening at the dinner table. Had the circumstances been different, if Eden and I had never dated, if we had simply been friends, I would probably still call Mr. and Mrs. Valmont every now and then to check on them and catch up. But the events that have taken place since will not allow it. So I keep that evening with them in their home in the fond recesses of my mind.

The doorbell rang and people began pouring in. Aunts, uncles, grandparents. There must have been at least ten family members there. Cynthia, Eden and I were the youngest among them. All seemed well put together. Men wore shirts tucked into knakis with fop vests or dinner coats. Women wore matching earrings and necklaces.

Boots' clumsy body knocked into people's knees. "Cynthia," Mr. Valmont commanded. "Put Boots away." Cynthia grabbed Boots' collar and led him into another room, shutting the door.

Mrs. Valmont joined the aunts as they nodded at me with smiles and whispered into Eden's ears.

I greeted the men and then made my way over to the aunts. One of Eden's relatives, Ginger, was a cute older woman; slender features, finely applied cosmetics, and her auburn hair neatly constructed into an updo style and pinned at the back of her head. She was married to a charming man who loved to say, "That's great! How 'bout that!" She grabbed my hand, pursed her lips, and gazed into my eyes. "Eden tells us you're a poet."

I darted my eyes to Eden and the other women. They all watched, biting back their laughter. Apparently this aunt was doing nothing unexpected. But I had some experience with this type of situation.

My dad was the youngest in his family and had six older sisters. Hanging out with a group of older women who are very comfortable in each other's company and speak their thoughts without reserve; there's nothing like it. A lot of fun.

When they gather and find a newcomer, especially a young, trusted man, if they're in the right mood, they'll have the greatest time with him. And any boy who's comfortable amidst older women can enjoy himself immensely. He must play along, show genuine interest in them, compliment them at times, never act cocky, and be charming and witty. I was no professional, but my aunts had afforded me much experience.

"I like to read poetry," I said. "But I'm not a poet."

"Well, I think that's hot," she said with a nod and an affirming grin.

I shook my head and could feel my face and neck flush red. All the women laughed, slapping their sides and hanging on each other. Eden was laughing too, but watching my eyes, making sure her aunt wasn't pushing me overboard.

Another aunt, a petite, short-haired blonde named Melissa, who used exaggerated hand gestures, said, "Okay, Ginger, he belongs to your niece and you're a married woman."

I raised my hands and answered, "Mrs. Ginger, if you were twenty years younger and single and I wasn't dating Eden, I'd perfect the art of poetry and write for you on a daily basis."

"Oh honey," Melissa interrupted, "you better be glad she's not twenty years younger and single; she'd teach you a thing or two." The women erupted in cackling laughter, rocking on their heels. Ginger's face turned red and she squeezed her lips together.

When Mr. Valmont announced it was time to eat, Melissa laid her hand on my shoulder and said, "That was great, Finn. She hasn't blushed in years."

Mr. Valmont whispered something into Eden's ear and she met him and her mother in the kitchen. Concerned, I stole a peek. Her parents appeared to be reasoning with her about something important. Arms crossed, Eden was listening with a stunned expression. Two of her uncles and another aunt interrupted me.

"We heard you're a professor," one of the uncles said.

"Oh, no sir. Uh, not yet." I glanced in the kitchen again, but they had moved to the opposite side of the room.

"How do you know Eden?" the aunt asked.

"We—uh . . ."

"There she is!" the uncle said.

Eden wrapped an arm around me and leaned her head on my shoulder. I kissed the side of her head.

"You okay?"

She didn't look at me. She nodded, but looked away.

Mr. and Mrs. Valmont rejoined the party with smiles, knowing they must entertain guests. But something was wrong. Perhaps a family issue? Did I do or say something wrong? I wasn't sure.

"Let's eat," Mr. Valmont announced, and all gathered around the table and joined hands. Mr. Valmont, with the customary ease of having done something a thousand times, lifted his wife out of her wheelchair and sat her in the chair beside him. I took Eden's hand in mine and kissed it. She half-smiled at me but her eyes didn't shine as was normal. A light was gone.

Mr. Valmont led a prayer and we passed the food around the table and filled our plates.

"So, Finn," one uncle said. "Where will you be a professor?"

The house phone rang and Mr. Valmont excused himself. He disappeared around the corner, into the kitchen. I heard him say hello. Then he lowered his voice. Mr. Valmont peeked his head around the corner. "Eden."

Puzzled, Eden left her napkin in the chair and stepped into the kitchen. I heard her and Mr. Valmont whisper. There was a pause and they whispered again. Then Mr. Valmont said, "Just say hello." Mr. Valmont returned to the dining room with a forced smile. I heard Eden whisper hello. Boots appeared and nudged and licked my hand.

The uncle awaited a response, so I said, "Hopefully Vanderbilt." Then I eyed the entrance to the kitchen again.

"Eden tells us you're well-traveled," an aunt said.

"Finn's a missionary," her mother added. She sounded impressed. Everyone nodded and smiled.

"That's so nice, dear," the aunt replied.

"Thank you," I said.

Eden returned and sat down, laying her napkin in her lap. I waited for an explanation from her, but she wouldn't look at me. She pressed her lips together, looked down and ironed out her napkin with her hands.

I leaned toward her. "Hey," I whispered.

"And what did those experiences teach you?" the aunt asked.

Boots licked my hand again. When I didn't pet him, he bit into my sleeve and tugged at me. I also realized I wouldn't be able to escape their inquisitive questions. I was the only newcomer to the group, and Eden's date. And they obviously loved and respected her and her family.

"To try to help without hurting," was my response.

"Could you elaborate?" the same aunt asked. Panic and frustration surged through my veins, but I swallowed.

"In the Caribbean," I began, "a woman refused to repair damages on her home because the summer approached and she said that's when missionaries come to rebuild the poorest homes. She chose to remain in her poverty so she could receive handouts. In West Africa, the missionaries gave the kids Western toys. And over time, the kids stopped playing with dolls their grandparents made for them.

"In my experience, we don't appreciate anything unless we work for it. When we receive handouts, our work ethic fails. And when we don't receive more, we develop a victimhood complex and entitlement issues. So we need to find ways to help, without hurting. That's what I meant. And I believe that's my mission. Do you ever think about things like that?" I had turned the question on them, hoping they'd leave me alone.

"Very good, Finn," Mr. Valmont said, nodding and smiling at me. "Very good."

Boots barked at me, for not petting him. Everyone laughed and returned to eating.

"Cynthia," Mr. Valmont commanded again. "Put Boots away and lock the door."

Eden and I settled into our seats for our return flight home. She leaned over and nuzzled her face into my shoulder, holding my arm with both hands. "My parents really liked you," she said, looking at me like I was a prized find.

"They're good people," I said. "Your dad, if someone can't get along with him, then it's their fault. He's great. One of the kindest men I've ever met. And your mom. She has this aura about her. She's very wise. I can see why your dad fell for her. It seems like she's seen a lot."

Eden smiled and nodded. "She has. She's a good mom. I have a great family."

"You do. Your sister loves you too."

"I know," Eden said and looked away.

We sat there in silence for a while, and I sensed Eden was reliving the dinner again in her mind. She stared out the window a lot. At times, she closed her eyes and acted as if she was asleep. Soon she let go of my arm, and her hands folded in her lap.

When she woke, she was quiet and distant. When I asked her if everything was okay, she smiled and said, "Yeah," and thanked me for my concern. She was warm to me again and held my hand. I kissed the top of her head and breathed in the scent of her. But then anxiety flickered in her expression, and she averted her eyes, as if something terrible was gnawing at her.

"What happened back there?"

"It's nothing," she said. "Just my parents."

"What?"

"I don't want to talk about it."

I thought maybe I had met her parents too soon. In America, meeting the parents is something that isn't normally arranged until much later in a dating relationship. Though it's not that way in other countries, meeting the parents is a big deal in American culture. I knew couples who had dated for two years and the boyfriend didn't meet the parents until he was ready to ask permission to marry their daughter. So, I thought maybe Eden felt things were just moving too fast.

When we arrived back at her apartment that night, she wouldn't look me in the eye. I kissed the side of her head.

"You still don't want to tell me?" I asked.

Loud, drunk students yelled and laughed down the hall. Two girls and three guys stumbled at the door. One of the girls fumbled with her keys as she slid one into her lock and said something indecipherable. Then the door shut behind them, smothering the noise.

When I looked back at Eden, her lips quivered and tears puddled in her eyes.

"Just stuff with my family."

"Tell me."

Then she hugged me, tight.

"I can't. But know I love you. Do you believe that?"

"I love you, too," I said. "Hey—"

"No matter what happens with my family or when we graduate, just know I love you."

"But—"

"Please, don't," she said. "Just tell me you believe me."

"I believe you."

She kissed my lips, not with passion, but as if she was saying goodbye.

The next day I purchased coffee in the cafeteria between classes. I saw Chaplain Metcalf in an opposite line, buying lunch.

"Chaplain Metcalf," I called, striding toward him.

"Finn!" he said, shaking my hand.

"It's good to see you. What are you doing here?"

"Oh, fundraising and meetings, and seeing an old friend." Dr. Daniels and his wife joined us.

"Hey, Doc," I said, shaking his and his wife's hands.

"Hi, Finn," they said.

"You guys having lunch?"

"Yeah," Chaplain Metcalf replied. "You want to join us?"

"I can't. I have class. Thanks, though."

"Yeah, we're talking about Pepperdine's involvement with the clinic. So it'll be exciting."

"I know it will. And I'm glad to hear it," I said. "You've come to the right university if you're looking for servant-minded leadership."

"We figured that out a long time ago," Chaplain Metcalf answered, smiling.

"I'll let you guys have lunch. It was good seeing you," I said. "Thanks for everything you do."

"You too," he returned.

That afternoon, during one of Dr. Daniels' lectures, I checked my phone, but still no missed calls or texts from Eden. I had tried calling her earlier but only got her voicemail. I stepped out of class and tried calling her again, but no answer. "Hey," I said into her voicemail. "I still haven't heard from you. Let me know you're okay."

Dr. Daniels opened the door. "Finn," he said, and motioned me back into class.

Later that night, rain fell outside as I studied at my desk. Having still not received word from Eden, I called Joanna.

"Hi, Finn," Joanna said. "You need to come over."

"What happened?" I asked, shooting out of my chair.

"Just come over."

I burst out the door with my coat and keys. The rain poured. I don't even remember driving to her apartment, really. But I remember banging on the door with all my clothes soaked and water running into my eyes.

When Joanna opened the door to let me in, Katie stood behind her in the living room with her arms crossed. Deep down, I knew whatever was wrong, she was a part of it. Books and study materials were strewn on the dining room table. They had been studying. Joanna handed me a folded note, written in Eden's handwriting.

Dear Finn, I moved home to Colorado. If you ever loved or respected me, please do not contact me. Just know I love you. I'm so sorry.—E

The *E* was cut off, as if she was overcome before she could finish writing her name. I pushed past Joanna and Katie to Eden's room. Her door was closed and I burst in. Empty. The bed and dresser were still there, because they belonged to Pepperdine. But she left no trace of ever having lived there. All other belongings were gone. I rushed into her art room. Empty.

"What happened?" I demanded, charging at Joanna.

"She wouldn't tell me," Joanna answered, solemnly.

"When did you last see her?"

"Last night. She was distraught but said she felt sick and was going to bed."

"And today?"

"I never saw her."

"What about this letter? You've had this the entire time and you didn't tell me?"

"I found it after class. On the counter."

"Why didn't you call me?"

"I was confused," she said, growing panicked. "I didn't know what to tell you."

I shot my eyes at Katie. "Did you have something to do with this?"

"No!" she said, shocked at my accusation.

Stunned and helpless, I wadded up the letter, threw it into Eden's room, and left.

When I entered my apartment, Ryan and Oz jumped from their chairs. Ryan, who was on his phone, hung up.

"We just heard," Oz said, stunned.

"If you guys know anything, tell me now," I said, curtly.

"We don't know anything," Oz replied.

"Ryan, does Joanna know?"

"No. She's being honest," he answered.

"I don't want to hear Eden's name mentioned ever again, unless someone knows exactly what happened to her," I snapped. I entered by room, slammed the door behind me, reared back and punched my fist through the wall.

Chapter 4

As the weeks progressed, with the obsessive-compulsive feelings the loss of a lover brings, the loneliness from their vanquished presence and all those loving feelings that refuse to leave, I felt as though I was mourning the death of a loved one.

Eden's parting was as final as a slammed door. She never called, never wrote; she was gone. So I flew home to Tennessee for the weekend to visit with Grandpa and be with my parents. It's the only place in the world where I can clear my head. Life always makes sense when you're home. I had called Grandpa from California just before I left and filled him in on the story. He assured me that tea and some time together awaited me.

Back on the farm, a storm had felled a tree near the pasture. And though Dad had sawed it into firewood, the brush needed piling, and the trunk pieces stacked for winter. "Would you mind helping me with the brush after I finish feeding the cows?" Dad asked.

Of course I wouldn't mind.

During my time home, I reflected on my life before Pepperdine, and the inner conflict now occurring. I thought about how cozy, lovely and homey our farm and hometown was.

Grandpa would go for strolls alone through the

pastures where meadowlarks and grasshoppers flitted about, where rabbits constructed their havens, and thick-coated coyotes and red-tailed foxes sniffed and searched them out.

The spring and summer air was always filled with butterflies and bumble bees, and scents of wild honeysuckles. Bluebirds and sparrows competed for nests in the oaks, and redheaded woodpeckers rattled the trunks and shafts of the sugar maples. At night, lightning bugs dipped in the air, and crickets and tree frogs sang anthems that could be heard through closed windows.

As a child, I spent crisp spring afternoons wading along Reedy Creek just beyond the field. Then came the heavy breeze in the autumn, blowing the almond-brown, auburn, sugar-yellow and apple-red leaves into the creek, providing rafts for dragonflies. In winter, the snow upon the wood became an eerie deep, and the occasional gliding of an owl would be spotted from our bedroom. Then, to spend an afternoon walking in a snowy wood and find a scarlet-red cardinal perched on a white limb, you would think God arranged that picture just for you.

My brother Caleb and I played hide-and-seek as children. Our cousins and friends from school rode their bikes to our house. We swam in Reedy Creek and then lay in the grass and pointed out animal shapes in the clouds. We licked the nectar off honeysuckles that grew in the woods behind our home, and at night, captured lightning bugs in Mason jars.

We all worked in Grandpa's vegetable garden during the various seasons. In the summer, we planted rows of corn, radishes, potatoes, green peas, and green beans. Clusters of pea and bean shells hid in the vines. After the harvest, we sat before buckets, and shucked and shelled the vegetables to freeze for winter.

Then on Saturdays, we helped Dad mow the grass and trim the shrubs. Occasionally, after our work was done, Dad purchased a watermelon from the farmer's market, and we sat beneath the trees and ate the fruit while drinking iced sweet tea. When adult talk began, I would leave and lay under the shade trees, surrounded by the chirping and the buzzing of the country life, and stare up through the tree limbs and into the clouds. My mind wandered to distant lands I had only heard of in stories. And I promised myself that one day I would travel the world and be nice to people.

So during my visit home, after my duties were finished for Dad, I phoned Grandpa. He told me to come over when I was ready, and that a jar of sweet tea would be waiting beside my rocking chair on his front porch.

I knocked on Grandpa's door, opened the screen and stepped inside. His house was sky-blue-painted wood with a red door, like something out of a country magazine. The house had a wrap-around porch where sat the chairs and a fire pit. There, we talked into late winter nights by the fire with our tea in our hands.

Grandpa stuck to his routines. He spent his mornings on the back porch where he drank coffee, read the morning paper, and awaited deer that often grazed at the lawn's edge. He ran his errands and ended his afternoons on the front porch in one of the rocking chairs he'd crafted, sipping his tea and watching people pass by on their way into town.

"Grandpa?"

"Come on in," he called out from his study. Scents of fresh baked peach cobbler and banana pudding filled my nose. He pushed himself out of his chair and rose to hug me. "Welcome home, son." We embraced, and the sweet fragrance of pipe and aftershave on his neck reminded me I was safe. "Come, let's have some tea!"

From the fridge, he handed me the cold, sweating Mason jar of tea. Melting ice floated and a fresh cut lemon was pushed onto the glass's rim. The front screen door squeaked and shut behind us and we sat in our rocking chairs. In the trees near the driveway, blue jays cackled back and forth over a squirrel that had fallen into their nest.

"So, you finally fell in love," he said, smiling at me. There's one thing about Grandpa: when I talked, he could listen patiently, but when it was time for him to speak, he went straight to the point.

"Love," I answered. "I only knew her for a few months. What could have happened to her?"

"I don't know."

"No ideas at all?" I asked.

"I've never heard of anything like that. But whatever happened, it was serious."

"Is it possible to love someone after having known them only that long? Did I really know her at all?"

"You believe you loved her, don't you?"

"Yes, sir."

"Well, then, if that's your experience . . . It's what exists in the mind, whether people call it real or not. It was certainly real for you, wasn't it? Can we really place a time limit on falling in love? Sometimes it's like lightning. Other times it takes months or years. Love is action, not a feeling or something earned after years. It's something we choose to do. It's a decision. Self-sacrifice. When you walk an old lady across the street, you're being loving toward her. When you forgive an old friend, that's love. It's not the same kind of love that exists between you and your parents or the same love between a married couple. It's not the same love between a boy and his dog. But I know you loved her."

"How do you know?"

"Because you never told me about her. The deepest things for you, Finn, you keep to yourself until you're so comfortable and in control you find yourself sharing without even thinking about it. You take after your dad in that. He's always been that way. You're twenty-five years old. You've never really dated because you always seemed to know exactly who you were looking for. It sounds like this girl really made an impression on you."

I rocked and nodded my head, quiet.

"But don't get me wrong," Grandpa added. "Since you never experienced love with a woman, you don't know how it changes over the months and years. It's always perfect in the beginning. But, you know it's over now. Whatever happened, you must do as she asked. Stay away from her."

A stabbing pain shot through my chest. I thought about just thanking him and leaving. Grandpa would understand. But I loved and respected him too much. He didn't mean any harm by those words, but I felt nauseous, bitter, like all hope in the world, which had once been my foundation, was now broken, torn, and taken from me.

"Why would God bring her into my life, knowing how I would interpret it all, only to take her away?"

"Why, why, why," he said. "Finn, sometimes life just is. Let me tell you a story about a bird named Birdie."

As a child, when Grandpa would start off his

conversations with, "Let me tell you a story," I would grumble and sink into my chair. "Just tell me what you want me to understand," I would say. But Grandpa never made it that easy. He used stories as parables and oftentimes, depending on the circumstances, answered my questions with questions. Over the years, I had learned to just be quiet and listen, knowing the lesson or answer would come eventually. So I adjusted my seat and waited.

"There once was a little boy named Sam," Grandpa began. "He loved his pet bird, Birdie. He found her when she fell out of her mother's nest. Sam took Birdie home and raised her until she could fly. Months passed, and when his dad came home and told Sam it was time to open the cage and free Birdie, Sam cried because he knew Birdie would leave.

"Sam's father knelt down on one knee to be at eye-level with his son and replied, 'Sam, what's best for Birdie?'

" 'If I let her go, will she ever return?' Sam asked.

" 'That's a risk. But it must be her decision. If she is meant to be yours, she'll return.' Sam turned and walked over to the cage, opened its door, and immediately, without hesitation or even a thank-you, Birdie flew into the woods and out of sight. Sam turned and ran into his daddy's arms, weeping.

"The message is, if the bird is meant to be yours, it'll come back. The worst thing about grief, Finn, is that the passing of time is the only remedy. And that's what makes it hard." The old grandfather clock chimed in the living room. "Make sure to swing back by the house before you go to California tomorrow. If I'm not here, check the jar on the desk. I might leave you something, okay?"

We walked into the kitchen and enjoyed a generous helping of cobbler and pudding. And for the first time since Pepperdine, he made me laugh, retelling old stories from the "good ol' days." I placed my jar in the sink and acted like I was going to wash it, because I knew Grandpa would slap my hands and tell me he'd do it. So I acted, he slapped, I left the jar in the sink, and we hugged each other goodnight.

Ten hours later, I was back at Grandpa's, but he was out on his morning walk. So I stepped into his study and saw a letter sitting in the Mason jar on the nearest corner of his desk. Mom and Dad were waiting in the car, to take me to the airport. So I stuffed the letter in my pocket, wrote Grandpa a quick note, *I love you,* on scrap paper and dropped it in the jar. When I got back into the backseat and we began our trip to the airport, I waited for Mom and Dad to settle into conversation with each other. Then I pulled out the note and read Grandpa's words.

Finn,

I know right now, all that is visible is seen through the lenses of loss and pain. So, I'm not sure the words I say to you will resonate. But know that feelings just are. Experience them. Don't deny them or push them away. If you do, they will come out through other avenues like short-tempers and sharp answers to friends and loved ones who don't deserve to be mistreated.

We do not deny our experiences, good or bad. We must embrace them. They are a part of who we are. The point is to keep from dwelling on the past or holding on to the bad times. This way, we don't lead ourselves into resentment, cynicism and bitterness. If we want to get angry and scream at God because we think it's His fault, that's okay. He can handle our anger. God might not appear to care, but He does. He promises us that. We can give up on Him and walk away, but how much better off will we be?

You might believe that you must stop loving Eden, but that's not true. We can love even when we know that love will never be returned. We are allowed to love someone even if that person is gone. What we miss is their presence, but that doesn't mean we must stop loving them. As Maclean wrote, it is those who we love the most who so often elude us. But we can still love them. We can love them completely, without complete understanding.

Loving is not the same as holding on because "holding on" implies that we hope the loved one will come to their senses and return. Love is an action based on free choice despite the consequences. Love only becomes painful when it demands something in return. And though it may take time, you will find joy in loving those who might not even be aware of your love.

So I must ask you, "Do you believe God loves you?" When you can answer yes and understand that answer, you will have found the security you need. You'll step into that light and discover all other lights are dim in comparison. Though affirmation from family and friends brings healing, nothing compares to the healing and encouragement from the affirmation that you will find in His words.

Understand, son, that we can only help those who have hit rock bottom when we ourselves have seen existence through that same lens. Therefore, you can use the pain you've experienced to ease the pain in others. This does not mean God purposefully inflicts pain or is the author of loss, nor does it mean that every time we experience loss or pain that God is behind the cause. But it does mean that God can take the bad things and turn them into beautiful things. But that takes time. It cannot happen overnight.

What's important is to remain close to Him, not run from Him or give into temporary, fleeting pleasures to try to help deal with the pain within. Life without instruction will only cause you additional pain. So be warned, son. Don't run away from Him during this time. Talk to Him, embrace Him. We must remind ourselves that there are always more questions than answers when it comes to life and the Infinite.

I'm sorry that I have rambled on and on, but I sometimes must write out my thoughts before I share them with you. In my old age, it helps me articulate what I want to say. Know Clayton, I love you. Your parents love you, your brother loves you, and above all, God loves you. Dwell on these things. Hang in there and stay encouraged. As the old saying goes, "This too will pass."

—Grandpa

I folded the letter and stuffed it in my coat pocket and stared out the window at the countryside.

"Son," Dad said, lifting his face so he could gain a clearer view of me through the rearview mirror. "You sure are quiet back there. You've been quiet all weekend."

Mom turned her head to the side. "You sure are. You've been quiet over the last few years but you've never been this quiet. Why?"

I returned my eyes to the moving pastures outside my window. "Life's easier when you're quiet."

PART II

With tears in her eyes, Eden tucked Finn's novel under her arm and stepped to the sliding glass door that overlooked London. She stared into the sky streaked with colors of peaches and violets. The images from Finn's novel, and her own memories from Pepperdine, replayed before her.

Her phone rang. *Joanna.*

"Hey," Eden answered, opening her door and stepping onto her deck. Swallows swooped and darted at the corners of London's towers.

"Are you finished?" she asked.

"Am I a bad person?" Eden replied, tears spilling over her cheeks.

"No, Eden," Joanna answered. "You're one of the best people I know. There are few women who would have sacrificed the way you did."

"I thought Finn hated me."

"No, he loved you. You need to finish the book. Especially with Pepperdine happening this weekend."

"Are you sure Finn will be there?"

"Ryan said he might."

Eden nodded, wiping the tears away. "Okay," she answered.

"Call me when you finish reading it," Joanna said.

"I will."

And at that, Eden stepped across the threshold, slid the door closed behind her, and re-entered Finn's memoir.

Chapter 5

Back at Pepperdine, my memories of Eden and me together followed me everywhere. I retreated to Dietrich's every day, and when I wasn't studying for school, I tried to lose myself in the writings of C. S. Lewis, Henri Nouwen, and Thoreau. When my eyes were spent, I set the books down and stared at the fountain, where birds and children played in the water.

I hadn't thought it was humanly possible to love a woman so much. To not care if she read my thoughts, past or present, to *want* her to read my thoughts. To wonder how I could have lived a life without knowing her, and now, how to live without her. Life became like a hazy dream where all exists amiss and out of place.

She was my first love. My only love. During my time with her, life was beautiful, and after, I wondered how I had ever lived without her.

Oz would often zip into Dietrich's for a coffee or tea, and if he had time, he grabbed a chair under one of the sun umbrellas. That day, he was sitting beside me, reading a newspaper.

"Oz, why do I always want to just come down here and read?"

"Well, you're at peace," he replied. With a flip of the newspaper, he continued reading.

But I'm not at peace, I thought. I come here to escape the world, Pepperdine, existence itself, to transcend time, to get lost in reading. Nothing quiets me. Not solitude, reading, or even prayer. It's like there's an unknown thing left undone that I can't put my finger on. It eats at me, and I feel like I'm wasting my life away.

Before I met Eden, I would have nightmares of street kids rocking back and forth in fetal positions, holding their abdomens because of bad food or drugs. Those dreams had disappeared after I met Eden, and now they returned. I would fall asleep, exhausted from studying and fighting to keep Eden out of my mind, have the nightmares, and then wake in the morning, feeling like I never slept at all.

I thought of all sorts of avenues to distract me. Against my better judgment, I got drunk a few weekends in a row and made out with three different girls within a two-day period. My search for cheerfulness or to simply feel again left me feeling emptier. I then understood how people got hooked on drugs and alcohol. Anything to escape reality, for just a moment of peace, or to feel alive again.

The nights were the worst. My apartment was always cold, no matter what the thermostat read. My window and half my walls faced the ocean, so coastal winds constantly pushed against my room. My pillowcase and sheets stayed cold and crisp when not pressed firmly against me. The quiet, and the glow from my phone and computer, somehow added to the loneliness.

If I had been at Grandpa's, at least I could have heard the clock tick-tocking and feel the warmth of a home filled with years of laughter and family gatherings. And know he's in the opposite room.

During my time abroad, I felt alone at times. But it wasn't until after Eden was gone that I felt completely lonely. I heard all those self-destructing, demeaning voices in my head saying, "Eden left because you're not good enough for her. You're not worth fighting for. Something's wrong with you. She didn't love you. You failed."

Overnight, wrinkles spread across my forehead. Little gray hairs sprouted amidst the brown in the sides of my hair. I hated women, I hated God, and I hated myself. If I had been a better person, I thought, she wouldn't have left.

I couldn't help but think I should have said something different in the park that day when we had our fight. Had that been an influence in chasing her away? I thought of the words I would speak to her if I could see and hold her again.

I would take her face in my hands and whisper to her, "It's okay if something happens in your personal life and you must leave. But if you ever feel like you must leave. But as the years pass and you remember our time together and you're at a place or with a person who makes you wonder what happened to the goodness in humanity . . . if you ask yourself if you were ever loved by someone other than those within your immediate family, the answer is yes. There was a boy you knew in college who loved you. A part of him will love you the rest of his life. No matter how much land or ocean or time separates the two of you, he will be there for you if you ever need him."

In all attempts to get over Eden, I went to the gym every morning and sprinted up the stairs that led through Pepperdine's campus, doing all I could to try to burn her out of my mind. One day, on my way to study, I passed by Dietrich's and saw the window's reflection of a guy staring back at me. I wondered how in the world he began looking so old. When I realized someone was watching me from the other side of the window, I moved on.

I saw Eden's face, like a movie reel replaying our time together. She laughed at my jokes and patted my knee because we both knew she got me when no one else could. Once, we'd both shaken our heads at each other when we over-heard a Malibu guy ask for his gourmet coffee drink to be remade because it was stirred instead of shaken.

Then there was the time we'd met a girl on Third Street in Santa Monica as she was passing out invitations to a Hollywood strip club. She had just moved from Michigan after her brother was killed in a motorcycle accident. Now, she was handing out advertisements for the club, using that money to help pay her living expenses while she attended cosmetology school. Eden and I went into a local bookstore and bought the girl C. S. Lewis' book, *A Grief Observed*, which Lewis wrote after a loved one died. When we gave it to her as a gift, the girl cried.

I had never served in missions alongside a woman I cared for. Eden wanted to work with orphans and so did I. I was beginning a new, beautiful chapter in life. I finally had a helpmate.

And then, she vanishes.

I passed my master comprehensive exams at the end of the semester, signed my name on my final essays, and walked outside toward the cafeteria, passing by the fountain.

I needed coffee.

Dr. Daniels trailed me. "Finn," he called.

I turned and faced him, stroking my cheeks, a habit of mine when I'm worn out. "Hey, Doc," I said with a forced smile. We shook hands, and he patted me on the back. He seemed anxious, but that was him. He had students to teach, papers to grade and speeches to make.

"Have you got plans after this semester?"

"No, sir. I'm wanting to go for my Ph.D. at Vanderbilt."

"You worked with street orphans in Mongolia, right?"

"Yes, sir."

"For how long?"

"Just a summer."

He pointed toward a cement bench beside the fountain. "Well, do you have somewhere you have to go or can you sit for a minute?"

"No, it's okay. I have some time." We sat and I rested my elbows on my knees. "What's up?"

Dr. Daniels leaned back then sat forward, clasping his hands. "There's a street children's mission in Kenya, called Made in the Streets. One of their missionaries was killed last month in Nairobi. Some rebels have gone into the slums and tried to kidnap kids to make them soldiers. When the parents tried to intervene, they were killed. Apparently, a lot were killed. There were already kids living on the streets, but now the number's in the hundreds."

I hid my face in my hands. I knew what was coming, and I didn't want to do it.

"The other missionary left after it happened, and now it's just an older couple overseeing the mission with help from some of the former street kids. There's all these kids on the streets without food and they've taken to sniffing glue. William and Jacey Colburn, the missionaries, they need someone to help until they can find some people full-time. They asked me if I knew anyone, and I told them I might."

He knew I would do it, somehow, and he knew I needed to.

"Finn, they could really use your help."

I rubbed my face and hair. "Doc, I'm tired. I wasn't planning to pursue my Ph.D. until next year because I'm burned out. I need a break."

"What's wrong?"

"I don't want to talk about it."

He patted his knees. "Well, if you ever want to talk, let me know."

"I will."

"Listen," he said. He almost stood, but sat tight again. He rubbed his thumb into his palm. "You've been to Africa."

"That was North Africa," I retorted. "Arab-Muslim territory. It's not the same."

"There's no one else, Finn. I've called every-one I know and they're either busy with other missions or they can't. You can do this. It's just for the summer. The funding's already taken care of. It'll get you there and even cover your expenses during your stay."

"Doc," I said. "You know as well as I do there are no guarantees this is just a summer thing. I get over there and spend the summer and when it's over, there might not be replacements. I leave anyway and the team and all the kids think I deserted them."

Dr. Daniels looked at his watch. "Finn, you've got to do what you've got to do. But let me say this one thing. You're young, single, and you have no plans right now. If you're as burned out as you think you are, then Africa will bring you healing. There's no deadlines, no papers, no speeches and no cell phones. You're just there helping as a volunteer with a stipend. No one will blame you when you leave, because they'll all know it's just for the summer. So if you change your mind, call me as soon as you can, okay? But I have to meet a student, so I need to go."

I nodded, we shook hands and he walked away.

Later that evening, I peered out of my apartment window. Drescher T30. I could see for miles from that apartment; the lights flickering along the coast, the distant cities, the ocean and all of campus. Sights I once considered incredible now left a bitter taste in my mouth. There was nothing left for me in California. I wasn't ready to go home to Tennessee yet. But there was no way I was going to Africa, either. No way, I thought. They can find someone else.

I heard that ranchers in the Midwest take on hired hands during the seasons to help with chores. I could be surrounded by mountains or wheat fields as far as I could see, waking at dawn to a hearty breakfast and work during the day. Manual labor, if balanced, fuels the mind and soul. I could watch the pink sunrises and the purple sunsets. I could even go observe the wolves in Yellowstone, something I've always wanted to do.

The ranchers would become like family and they would mind their own business and never ask me deep questions or try to spark intellectual arguments with me, because their greatest concern would be whether God sent rain. They would even refrain from asking me questions too personal, like wanting to know all about my background, and why I was working on a ranch for minimum wage when I should be in school making something of myself.

Working on a ranch was the most fantastic idea I'd had in years. I wouldn't take any books other than a few novels. I could just enjoy a good story. And years later some old classmates would say, "Whatever happened to Clayton Fincannon?" And others would reply, "I don't know. I heard he went to work on a ranch somewhere out west and no one ever heard from him again."

That sounded wonderful.

The night before graduation, Oz called and said that there was a party for seniors on the president's back lawn. He and Ryan were going.

"I'm not a senior," I muttered. "And neither are you."

"No, but you and Ryan are graduating, and I'm going and others are going, so come on. We'll come pick you up."

I hadn't shaved in a few days. What does it matter if my face is rough or smooth? I'm not trying to impress anyone. I threw on some khaki pants and pulled out a dress shirt from beneath a pile of dirty laundry. I gave it the sniff test. It was wrinkled, badly, but I slipped it on anyway. I wore a hoodie too, unzipped, to help hide the wrinkles.

Ryan and Oz swung by in Ryan's green Camaro, and I hopped in. The sun was setting, turning the white buildings bronze. The warm air turned cool. We drove up the hill to the president's house, which overlooked the coast. The president greeted us in a navy-blue dinner coat, tan slacks and brown, shined shoes. His salt and pepper hair was parted neatly to the side. He shook our hands and gave us a welcoming smile. "Good to see you, boys. Go on out back. Everyone's out there."

White lights, strung through the trees, lit the back lawn. Men in bow ties stood behind tables covered with sparkling white cloth and adorned with crystal platters. There were refreshments and bowls of pink punch. As I stood at the fruit and salad bar, forcing myself to have cocktail conversations with seniors I'd never met, I realized how alone I actually was. And that I no longer belonged at Pepperdine.

As soon as my exams were finished, I arranged for Pepperdine to mail my diploma to Tennessee, and I returned home. I didn't even walk across the stage.

When I arrived back home to the farm, Grandpa and I stood on his back porch with our hands in our pockets, and I told him of Dr. Daniels' request.

"Let me grab my hat, and let's go for a walk." He stepped in and took his coat, hat and umbrella from the closet.

"You won't need your umbrella, Grandpa."

"Oh, I like to hold onto it. When I'm in town, I use it to beat off my lady admirers," he said, winking at me. Then he patted my back and squeezed my shoulder. Our feet crumpled the monkey grass, still sprouting from spring. The buttercups neared the end of their bloom and the wildflowers jiggled on their vines against the wind.

"So, son, any word from the girl?"

I shook my head.

"Mmmm," he said, nodding and folding his hands behind his back. His umbrella tapped the back of his shoe at every other step.

"Grandpa?" I asked. "Do you ever struggle with loneliness?"

"Are you serious, Clayton?" he answered. "If there's anything I've struggled with, it's been loneliness. In fact, one day at work, my secretary . . . oh, this was before you were born. She was a charming woman, a very good woman. She was like a sister to me after your grandmother passed. One day she handed me a book titled, *A*

Man with No Friends. I said, 'But I have friends,' and she said, 'No, you have mentors, you have pupils and you have acquaintances, but you don't have a real friend close by.' And she was right. My best friend lived over three thousand miles away, and we saw each other once a year."

"Is he still alive?"

"Oh, no, son. He passed years ago." Grandpa smiled at the memory of their friendship. "He was a good friend. We worked together in Africa. But when we returned home and got together, we always picked up right where we left off. Still, seeing one another once a year, it wasn't enough. Even though your parents live down the road and my life in this world is nearing its end, and I believe I've lived it to its fullest, I still feel that loneliness periodically.

"You know, there's something very special about finding someone who can relate to us, who for a period of time brings contentment and relieves us of all loneliness and despair. When we see people as gifts, rather than possessions, we learn to hold them rather than cling to them. My own experience has taught me that if you love people and let them be themselves in your presence, you'll never be short of friends. When you don't judge people and you instead allow them space to grow, they'll always remember you because they know they were loved unconditionally. Do you have a best friend, Clayton?"

"Yes, sir. Ryan, you know, my friend from Pepperdine. And I have a friend named Oz. But now that I've graduated, we won't see each other as much. But when we do get together, it's like we never left."

"That's exactly how we were too. When we would talk on the phone, we knew we would need a space of time because we'd take forever. But I know that loneliness you're talking about, Clayton. I know what it's like. Other than these short visits you've made home, including the holidays, how long have you been away?"

"Six years."

Grandpa stopped and looked at me. I paused too, knowing this meant he had something important to say. His body was frail but when he stood with his chin up like that, staring into my eyes, I had no choice but to respond with complete honesty. He could level me with that look. I was like a vulnerable child every time he did it.

"What do you want, Clayton?"

"Want from what?"

"From life. What do you want?" he said.

I looked down at the grass and skimmed my shoe across it. "I want to come home."

Grandpa hung his arm around my neck and anchored me into a soft headlock. "Son, you can come home anytime you want." He smiled down at me and patted my back, pushing me forward to continue our walk. "Being home for a while would be good for you. Back when you wrote me those letters from abroad, you spoke of the waterfalls and the crickets and pastures in Tennessee. That should tell you something. Pay attention to where your mind goes when it wanders. It'll tell you a lot about yourself. Remember, when we don't live our lives in line with our values, we feel inadequate and unhappy. So it might do your heart and mind some good to just come home for a while."

"That's fine," I answered, "But when I'm home, my mind wanders to the foreign field, and I wish I was out there again. I wonder if it'll always be like this."

"You need to come home for a while. Take a break."

"You know what I'd really like? To be a professor. I'd like to attend Vanderbilt, teach college students, and give lectures like you did. I'd like to live close to home in a little house with a fireplace, half hidden by the woods. I want to take care of you and Mom and Dad and be near Caleb." I looked away and drew a deep breath. "I used to be the happiest kid I knew. So in love with life."

"What happened?"

"Disappointment. I didn't know the world was as mean and nasty as it can be."

"It's a hard lesson to learn, isn't it?"

"Yes, sir. There were times when I went on the foreign field because I truly cared about helping people. I wanted the adventure too, but it was more about them. But recently, the reason I've wanted to go is to help deal with the loneliness, because the experiences teach me, because they change me, turn me into a better person, a wiser person, a more grateful person for what I have. All pride leaves, and I feel free when I'm out there. But now, I don't want to go. I feel like I'm going more out of duty than out of love for the people."

"At least you're honest about why you go. But that doesn't mean you should stop going, Clayton, just because you feel your intentions aren't right. If you didn't go, they would remain without help."

"Things were fine for a while," I said. "I was finding ways to deal with the loneliness. I was studying, volunteering, traveling and reading. I kept filling the hole inside me with different things. Then last semester, I met Eden and she filled the rest. Loving her filled the hole. But when she left, she pulled everything out with her. It's like I have to start all over again." I stopped and stared out across the pasture. "Everywhere I go, eventually, I come to a place where I don't want to be here nor there. I feel lost."

Grandpa stood with me for a moment. A hawk dipped across our path and landed on a limb. Wood birds and bluebirds glided across the field, popped up, and landed on branches in the hollow.

"You know," Grandpa said. "A few years before I met your grandmother, I was working at the publishing company in Nashville. And there was this girl at Vanderbilt I met. And instantly, we just, *zooop,* came together. It was like we just held hands and said, 'Hi.' We dated for five months. Then one day, like that, she was gone. She'd dated a guy for three years, and she used me to get over him. It took me two years to get over her."

"I've never heard that story before," I said.

He affirmed it with a nod. "Well, I guess I've never had to tell it."

"Did you ever see her again?"

"Here and there. Your grandmother was with me each time."

"Was it awkward?"

"Boy, was it awkward!" he said, shaking his head and chuckling. "There aren't many missionaries who can do that kind of work alone, Clayton. I know God will bring you an amazing woman, because I know you'll be a great husband. He needs husbands and fathers like you. There'll be times when you'll be so mad at your wife you can't stand it. You don't think that's possible now, but it'll happen. But you'll have comfort in knowing she's there. No matter what happens, you come home, she's there. You had a fight? You wake up in the morning, she's there. One day, you'll be a missionary. Your wife will be a missionary. Your kids will grow up and be missionaries. And you may never be Summa Cum

Laude or Magna Cum Laude, but you love people and you're passionate."

"So what do I do? What steps do I need to take to get over her?"

"Be like Jesus." Grandpa closed his eyes and stuck out his hands, palms up, holding an invisible tray. "Father, into your hands I commit my spirit." Then he placed his hands in his pockets. "Remember, when Jesus was suffering, God didn't rescue Him. We're Easter people, Clayton. We're living in Friday, and like Jesus stayed in the tomb, you might have to be in the tomb for a few days, maybe a few months, or even years. But Sunday will come."

As we neared his back porch, he looked over at me with a cocked smile. "You know what you do when life deals you lemons, right?" He nudged me with his arm. "Huh?"

I smirked and gave a half-hearted smile. "Yes, Grandpa. Cut 'em up, throw 'em in a jar of sweet tea and thank God you're a southern boy."

"That's right," he laughed. "Now, how about a glass of that tea?" I nodded, and we stepped back into his home. He walked into the kitchen, while I leaned on the doorjamb. I watched him pull out the pitcher of tea from the refrigerator. He took two Mason jars from the cupboard and poured until the tea reached the jars' rims.

"You know when I told you I'd been invited to spend a summer in Africa?" I said.

"Hmm," he replied with his back turned to me, setting the pitcher back into the refrigerator.

"It won't be for just a summer. If I go, I'll be staying longer."

"I see," he said as he shut the cupboard doors. "How long?"

"Who knows? How many people do you know who are gonna rush over there when one of the missionaries was killed and rebels just slaughtered a bunch of people?"

Grandpa turned around to face me and leaned against the counter. "So you're going, huh?"

I looked away.

"That's quite a commitment if you choose to do it. Why do you want to go?"

"I don't!" I said, sharply. "But what will I do here, feed the cows and chickens? Stack brush once a week? Sit around and talk about the high school football team? I did want to go to the foreign field, but now I'm not sure. The only girl I ever loved didn't even have the decency and respect to tell me why she left. Other than Mom, Dad, Caleb and you, there's nothing keeping me here in the States. At least out there, I can have adventure and explore the world. I'll be back one day. I'm just really confused, and I need to get out for a while. I can come home anytime I want. I enjoyed working with orphans in Mongolia. I haven't forgotten it. Those are fond memories."

"Are you still having the nightmares?"

"Yes, sir," I said, suddenly calm. It meant a lot to me that Grandpa remembered that.

"Have you talked to your parents and brother about what you're going through?"

"I don't want to tell them. Ryan and Oz found out that I'm going to Africa, but that's all they know right now. And Mom and Dad have enough to worry about. It's better to just let them sleep soundly at night."

"So, from what I hear you saying, there's a part of you that wants to go to Africa, isn't there?"

"Yes, sir," I admitted, glancing back at the ground.

"Then tell me, why is it that you want to go?"

I felt emotion filling my throat and eyes but I swallowed it. "I'm tired. I'm so tired. And you went to Africa when you were my age. I want to be like you."

Grandpa chuckled under his breath and looked at the floor, embarrassed. "Son, you've been to places and seen things I've only dreamed about. You've done good things for good people. And you've done good things for bad people. And you will continue to do those good things. I was good at doing good things for good people, but not always for the bad. I wish I had. We're never sorry for showing kindness, even to people whom we feel don't deserve it. It's acting out in our anger and giving to people what we think they deserve that usually gets us into trouble. I'm very proud of you and Caleb. I'm very proud of the men you boys have become. I know your mom and dad are proud too."

I had always believed Grandpa was proud of me. I'm not sure why I needed to hear his words, but I did. I didn't want to need his affirmation, but his words were like water on a parched soul. He believed I was on a good path, that I was no longer a boy, but a man, and that I had what it took to do well in life. Every boy needs to believe that, needs to hear it from a grown man. A lot of healing took place right there in his kitchen.

"How will you get your funding?" he asked.

"Some people from a non-profit have already told Dr. Daniels that when he finds someone, they'll donate enough money to order the airfare and cover me for the summer. I thought I'd raise the rest later, if it's needed."

Grandpa nodded. "You do as much fund-raising as you can. Then I'll cover the rest, even if it's five years."

I nodded my head as I kept my eyes on the floor. Then I walked over to him and hugged his neck.

"Finn," he whispered. "The sun will shine again, son. The sun will shine again."

Chapter 6

The next morning, Ryan called and asked if he could join me in Africa. I said yes. Before he showed interest, I thought this would be a journey I would want to make alone. Why? I don't know. To bury my past, to get rid of my demons, to find a new life I guess. But it was good to have him onboard. The summer didn't seem so lonely now.

Ryan had graduated in theology. We entered Pepperdine at the same time, left at the same time, lived as apartment mates throughout and now we were headed to Africa. Years prior, he spent a summer in Zambia working with AIDS victims.

When I told my parents of our plans, they shared the concerns all loving parents would.

But Grandpa had written in a Mason jar letter,

> When you look back on your life when you're older, will you wish you had gone to Africa? Yes. So go. Do it while you're young and single. Because when you're older and married with kids, you won't be as mobile and free.
>
> Take a journal with you, and record your experiences and your thoughts. Years from now, it will be a priceless treasure for you.

While you're there, let the memories of those who love you encourage you during your hard times. They will get you through, like a warm blanket.

When I called William and Jacey in Kenya, William answered with a smile in his voice. "Clayton, we've been waiting for this call. We're thrilled you guys are coming. Are you and Ryan ready?"

"We're ready," I said. "I have some lessons for the street kids when you guys have activities for them. And I have some ideas on how we can get the street kids some warm meals every day until we can take them to the farm."

"That's great!"

"I've used stories from Aesop's fables with discussion questions at the end of each one. I thought the kids would like stories about animals."

Jacey clapped her hands in the background. "They will!"

"They sure will," William continued. "We'll have you guys teach some classes as well. English. Math. It's all third grade level stuff. We'll have the lessons waiting for you guys when you get here."

"Now how is it all set up? The farm, the center in Eastleigh . . . what is Eastleigh?"

"Eastleigh's the second largest slum in Nairobi,

the capital city. There's pollution, garbage, and drugs. That's where a lot of the street children are. The city center is a place where the kids come every Monday and get a warm meal. That's also the place where we decide who comes to the farm. They're chosen based on how much we know about them and if their families and government think it's fine. Then they come and live with us on the farm where they begin their new life."

"What about the killings that happened?"

"Well, things are progressing here. The rebels were from Uganda and were chased out by the U.N. Some of the kids escaped from the rebels and are living on the streets. Their parents were killed. But, some of the kids were living on the streets before the rebels even came. So you never know which kids are which until you talk to them. Kids are being sent to orphanages, farms. We're one among many. There's a lot of help here, but it isn't enough. The greatest need right now is to just get the kids off the streets, away from the drugs, and back into a normal life. School, warm meals and a safe place to sleep."

"And we're staying at the farm or in the city?"

"On the farm," William said. "You'll have your own apartment in the boys' center on the farm, and you'll supervise them. But there will be days when you will go into Eastleigh and visit the bases where the street kids hang out. The bases are street corners and alleys where they hang out and sleep.

And you'll spend time with them and invite them to the city center. You'll have a good time, and we're excited that you boys are coming."

"I heard Al-Queda is in Eastleigh too," I said. "How's that going?"

"Yeah, they're there," William answered. "Refugees come from everywhere, even Somalia. A lot of them live in Eastleigh. But we've been there for years, and we've never had any trouble out of them."

"What about the boy that was killed?"

"Boy?" William replied, surprised at my comment. "He wasn't a boy. He was a man. Full grown, about forty-five years old or so. I guess you heard. He hadn't been here long. He came from Wisconsin to help. We told him to stay out of Nairobi after sundown, but he didn't listen. We told him that multiple times. He was volunteering in the city center and was on his way to catch a *matatu*, a mini bus, when he was stabbed and robbed."

I was silent for a moment, realizing the impression given by Dr. Daniels was different.

"Are you scared?" he asked.

"No, sir."

I heard William chuckle and I could tell he believed me.

Days later, I was reunited with Eden, in my dreams. We were in that old jazz club on Sunset

Boulevard near Santa Monica. I had discovered the club with some classmates, and I visited it after finals. I remember wishing Eden could have joined us. She would have loved it.

And, there we were. Just the two of us. The room glowed from the crimson lights on stage. A professional musician sat behind a piano, one plucked a bass, while another sighed through a soft trumpet. Candles and clusters of roses in crystal vases sat on the sides of each two-seated table. Eden and I were at one of those small tables, caressing each other's hands. The world was invisible. Just she and I, consumed by each other. She began to apologize, but I told her an apology wasn't necessary. I was just glad we were together again.

I leaned in and cupped her cheeks as she caressed my arm. She nudged her face deeper into the palms of my hands, making sure not an inch of her face was left unnoticed. She leaned toward me with her gentle, inviting smile. "What did you say to me every time we parted? 'You can do something for me,' what was it?"

"I used to say, 'Is there anything I can do for you before you go?' " Eden smiled at the memory. The darkness shrouded me and I woke to the buzzing of a fan, warding away mosquitoes. It was pitch-black and stuffy air filled my lungs, and I was reminded that I was somewhere I had never been.

Chapter 7

As the brick-red sun peeked over Lake Victoria in Uganda, the sounds of roosters, wild birds, and crickets filled the air. Ryan and I slept in a shed that had been converted into two bedrooms for visitors. I rolled out of my cot and walked through the backyard and into Mark's house to cook breakfast and take a shower.

Mark was a missionary who had served in Kampala, Uganda for the last three years. A family of expats lived in the house before him, but they left during a recent civil war. Mark's home stood on the edge of a mountain overlooking Lake Victoria, which borders Kenya, Tanzania, and Uganda. The backyard was a downward grassy slope, evolving into green hills with a mist that hovered above the lake.

Mark let us rest at his home before taking us to meet the medical missionaries, Darla and Ellen. Mark was the carpenter, with his own woodshop, where he spent most of his days. The three of them helped lead the church in Kampala and hired Ugandan staff to manage the church building and library. The library was famous in the city; home to one of the best seminaries in Uganda since professors from the States and the UK would fly in to teach classes.

William and Jacey asked that we first stop in Uganda and help Mark and the missionaries before traveling to Kenya. Projects were left unfinished since many expats fled because of The Lord's Resistance Army, the militia led by Joseph Kony. He was responsible for kidnapping children and turning them into child soldiers. Months prior, Eden and I had watched the documentary about it, *Invisible Children*.

Because of the constant civil unrest, the church was a safe house for many Ugandans. Some would come to the church and sit under the pavilion and talk and play chess or just hang out all day. During our first Sunday, rain pounded the pavilion's roof during the songs. The Christians would stand and dance, waving their hands in the air, clapping and shifting their weight from foot to foot. They sang despite their terrible past.

The Ugandans understood the effects of terror. They could recount tales of tribes coming in with machetes and garden hoes and wiping out entire villages of men, women and children. Every other man I met was a refugee from Congo, Burundi or Rwanda. They were eyewitnesses to genocide and often felt that the West stood aside and watched it all occur.

We had our routines. Ryan and I would run with Mark every morning at sunrise. Ugandans would greet us as they carried stalks of sugarcane over their shoulders, or balanced baskets of bread or rice on their heads. "Mazoongu! Mazoongu!" (white man) the children cried, pointing and smiling.

We worked with Mark, mixing concrete to patch potholes in the road near the church and seminary because the Ugandan government couldn't afford to properly care for the streets. One day, we rebuilt a dilapidated swing-set for the kids in the park. All that was needed was some extra screws, but no Ugandans had the screws or wanted to spend their limited funds on buying new ones.

Every day, I wore an old white t-shirt covered with oil and concrete stains, from years of working on our Tennessee farm. Yet when I stood beside the Ugandans, my shirt still shined. Their clothes were mostly donated from western charities and churches and had slowly made their way throughout Uganda.

Mark asked me to teach some literature classes at the seminary and instruct their students how to study the original culture of the author and the setting of the story. Ryan had studied culinary arts as an undergraduate, so he held afternoon classes where he taught the Ugandans kitchen hygiene and how to bake bread from scratch.

Our daily diet was fresh chicken, rice, beans, bananas, honey, bread and passion fruit. It was all raised, grown or baked behind someone's home. The average man only made three or four dollars a day, and people saved money for years just to build a block home. No wonder so many settled for a shanty made of scrap wood, mud and tin.

One of the Ugandan mission leaders, Isaac, invited us to his new home for a house warming. We traveled along bumpy red-dirt roads until we were in an area of town where the children and neighbors stared at us, smiling and whispering into each other's ears.

Isaac had built a cement block house with an outhouse and shower. One light bulb (that dangled from a loose wire in the kitchen) lit his house. No one brought gifts, because they couldn't afford gifts. Their gifts were themselves. Friends. Community. We sat in his living room, where we could barely distinguish each other's faces, and talked and sang Christian worship songs. Tears puddled in Isaac's eyes as he said, "I would like for us to take a moment to thank God for this home."

With his brothers, sisters, nephews, nieces and those from the church all sitting in the living room, they prayed a prayer of thankfulness while Isaac wiped his nose. I looked over at Ryan, who sat in the corner. He was leaning the back of his head against the wall with his eyes closed. Later that night, as we gathered in Mark's living room with Ellen and Darla to watch a movie, Ryan leaned over. "This place is awesome!"

Not long after his house-warming party, Isaac and I sat together in the church library, sipping *milk-tea,* a drink made of tea boiled in milk, while he recounted a history on Uganda's diplomatic evolution. "The British did not enter until the 1950s, so before then, we were still in tribes and living in villages. People still live in villages in the rural areas. There was always enough food and life was simple. We had gardens and hunting dogs. We tied bells around their necks so we wouldn't lose them. Families gathered around the fires and told stories to their children, about our past. Now the teens are too busy trying to act and dress like the people they see on television. A lot of the family life has been lost."

Kampala itself seemed like one large slum whose roadsides were open sewers. I wondered if perhaps the older ways were the best. What we Westerners call "progress," for Africans, could be "regress." Though I heard well-intentioned expatriates, missionaries and humanitarians speak of the progression of Uganda's medical provisions and technology, I still wondered if perhaps the industrious West should have left Africa alone.

That evening, Darla took me home after class with my students. She and Ellen were both in their forties and unmarried. Their only desire in life had been to live as wives and mothers, but they were sacrificing those dreams to serve in Uganda.

"You know, Clayton," Darla said with a smile. "You're an interesting guy."

I chuckled. "What do you mean?"

"You're hard to figure out."

"Why do you want to figure me out?"

"I like that kind of stuff. Personality tests, understanding people, that sort of thing. You can be in a joking mood at times but you also have a very serious side to you. Tell me about your past," she said, as we drove home.

"My past?"

"Tell me this," she said. "What's the greatest compliment you ever received?"

Life has taught me that when someone mentions certain things from their past, they reveal what matters to them, what they ponder, what troubles them. You are given insight into their worries, things which frighten them, what they value and what they keep with them through their life's journey. What someone does in their spare time and who they are when no one they know is around reveals a lot.

"My friend Dr. Daniels said I'm the kind of man he hopes his daughters will marry one day. That meant a lot to me, because it came from him." I told Darla about my family, about Grandpa, about how he once told me to ask myself what causes my heart to break, since that will give me insight into what my vocation should be in helping the world.

"What about you?" I asked. "Have you ever thought about returning home and getting married?"

"I planned to marry before leaving for the mission field," she said. "Then at the age of thirty, I knew if I kept waiting, I might never go. So I chose missions. I want to be married soon. I want to have children. As you get older, and you see that isn't happening, you wonder if it ever will. Do you have a girl back home?"

"There was one. But it didn't last long. Long enough to fall in love, though. I would have sacrificed it all for her. I wouldn't have returned to missions. I would have even stopped pursuing a Ph.D. if it meant being with her. If she had said, 'I want to move outside Colorado Springs to be near my parents,' I would have done it. I probably wouldn't be here."

"That's probably why it didn't work out," Darla said as she turned the steering wheel and we pulled into Mark's driveway. "You would've sacrificed it all. Maybe that's not what God has for you. If I were married, I wouldn't be able to do all the things I've been able to do. We don't see it at the time, but I think God does things to keep us from messing up our own lives. He's saved me from all kinds of mistakes."

That night, before I went to bed, I sat with the watchguard, Bernard. He worked for Mark and attended the church. The expats and missionaries hired men from the church to be their watchguards, and they hired women to serve as housemaids. It wasn't because the missionaries were spoiled. They did it to provide jobs for the poor. Africans assumed all white people were rich. They would have considered Mark rude if he hadn't hired someone.

Bernard and I sat on upside-down buckets and talked through the night. He told stories about growing up in Africa and the atrocities he witnessed between the Tutsi and Hutu.

"That wasn't the first time it's happened," he said. "You know, the massacre back in '94. Since the 1950s there have been six genocides. There were massacres against the Tutsi twice in the 70s, twice in the 80s, one in '93 and then another one in '94. That movie, *Hotel Rwanda*, just depicts one of them. I came from Burundi to Uganda. You see, the Hutu and Tutsi are not just in Rwanda. They are all over East Africa. There are more Tutsi and Hutu in Burundi than there are in Rwanda.

"So when one tribe starts to kill the other, word spreads quickly and everyone joins in. I've witnessed entire villages wiped out. People who have known each other for years; they might be your next door neighbor, or maybe they are living in the village down the road. And you can hear them clanging their machetes and garden hoes. They are coming over the hill saying, 'Hey! We are coming to kill you!' So everyone gathers and grabs any weapon they have to protect their families and homes. I have seen babies, infants, children, put in barrels and burned alive."

"Burned alive?"

"Yes," he said.

"But in barrels?"

"They stick the children in the barrels and seal them and sit them over a fire. The heat kills them. It burns them. Those men who did that knew those children all their lives. They walk down the street and see them playing. When you think back on it, you really want to just sit down and cry."

"What started all of this?"

"The Hutus were once under the Tutsi. They were like slaves. When the Belgians came in the 1950s, they say, 'Why do you let the Tutsi rule you? Fight them.' That started it. Then anger was passed down. In 1993, the President of Burundi was a Hutu. And he said, 'I know the Tutsi will kill me. When they do, I want all the Hutu to kill them off.' And then he was assassinated. But some people think his own people, the Hutu, killed him and blamed it on the Tutsi."

"How can you tell if someone is Tutsi or Hutu?"

"You can tell by the way they look, their facial features. You just know. Not long ago, a bus was pulled over and the men outside were Hutu, and they separated all the ones who were Tutsi to the side, just by looking at them. If you can't tell, you look at their papers. Then they killed them."

"Which are you?"

"I'm Tutsi."

"But what if someone is part Tutsi and part Hutu?" I asked.

"You find out what their father was. If the father was Tutsi, then you are considered Tutsi and you die."

During further interactions with Bernard, I learned that he had lost seven family members in the massacres. Bernard then joined a protest in the square of a university, against the Burundi government, for not putting an end to the wars. Many of the students were arrested and some were tortured. "After that," he said. "I left Burundi." And that was how he came to Uganda.

I took out my journal, which I had packed before I left, and recorded my experiences and reflections by the candlelight.

In the church at Kampala, there are refugees from Burundi, Sudan, Congo, Somalia and Rwanda. There are more refugees in Uganda than Ugandans. Isaac told me that last year the USA donated some $1.2 million for the AIDS relief work here, and it was all stolen by governmental officials and used for other things. Many Ugandans say that the money went into their pockets. I would not doubt it. The government here cancelled the exporting of their crops, even though agriculture is Uganda's best money earner, because "the rich people, the farmers, needed to be controlled."

The rebel militia in northern Uganda, The Lord's Resistance Army, tried to overthrow the Ugandan government, and has kidnapped children and turned them into soldiers. Their leader, Joseph Kony, fled to Congo in 2003 and has recently commanded his army to stop the abductions. This place is just a mess.

Then there were the genocide wars. There's a Catholic church building in Rwanda where the Tutsi people fled to escape the Hutu killers. They considered the church a haven. The killers came to the church building and told the priest that if he let them have the Tutsi, they would spare him and his family. So he gave in. I hear the church building is now a memorial; the bones of the victims still remain inside like a Holocaust museum. I was thinking the other day about why that priest made this decision. Would a locked door stop an angry mob that had been killing men, women and children? And if the priest believed that the people would die no matter his decision . . . People around here speak with so much scorn toward that priest, but if they had been in his position, would they have made a different choice?

Despite all that is taking place, there is so much joy in these people. They all come and hang out at the church building and talk and laugh. On Sunday, there are songs and prayers with more enthusiasm than I have ever seen in the States. Through teaching and serving in construction, I have developed a relationship with many of them and they now greet me with, "Clayton! Ha ha ha!" and they hug me or give me behind-the-back-high-fives. As far as lighter experiences go, we have eaten roasted grasshoppers, roasted goat, we rafted the Nile River, I have thrown roasted bananas to baboons, Ugandans have often called out to Ryan (who has grown a full beard and mustache) saying "Jesus!" while throwing their heads back in laughter. And I have been offered a man's sister for a price.

On a visit to a medical mission with Ellen, I stood near a river at the Ugandan/Congo border and filmed two shepherd boys. They live in a grass and mud hut. Every day's the same: life in the sub-Sahara taking care of the garden and animals. No cars, no city, little money, if any. All they have is their family, their neighbors and their livestock. Their lives revolve around these things. If they had any questions for me, I doubt they would ask much about America since they're without a radio, television, or a computer. I imagine them asking something along the lines of, "Do you fish?" or "Have you ever killed a croc?" And I cannot help but wish that I were a little more like them.

As our visit to Uganda concluded, Mark and I took Ryan to the airport, and we hugged our goodbyes. I would be traveling on to Kenya, and Ryan would return to Pepperdine to begin his position as an academic advisor.

Mark dropped me off at a bus stop in Mbale for my journey to Nairobi. A newcomer to Uganda named Jimmy, who was also a recent graduate from Pepperdine, would be joining me on the journey to the street children's farm in Kenya. He had a thick build, was of Asian descent and had been raised in California. It was nice to have him along since the bus ride was a good thirteen hours.

Night fell during our trip. The moon shone through the window, and the bus jarred us and shook as if it was about to fall apart. The bus occasionally passed a streetlight, and a soft wave of light would pass through, allowing us to see our neighbor's faces. About eight hours into the trip, I opened my backpack and pulled out a traveler's mix of nuts and dried fruit I had prepared before leaving the States. To keep from having to handle the food with my hands, I turned the bag upward and let the nuts and fruit tumble into my mouth. I brought the bag down as a light passed through the window. I noticed every African on the bus staring at me.

I suddenly realized they had probably not eaten all day, and possibly nothing the day before, either. If I had a suitcase full of traveler's mix, I would have passed it out to everyone. But all I had was what was in my hand. A wave of humiliation swept through me, leaving me feeling ashamed. I rolled the plastic bag as slowly as I could to keep it from crackling. I pushed it into a hole in my backpack and sunk down into my seat and stared out the window, chewing in slow motion, wishing I could disappear.

At midnight, the bus stopped at the Kenyan border, and all the passengers were asked to get out. Men with notepads huddled around the bus, all of them fighting for our attention. They were money changers. We approached what looked like a large concession stand and waited in line to purchase a visa to enter Kenya. The air was tight with the sharp odor of hundreds of unbathed, sweaty men bidding, yelling, and arguing.

We had to exchange our Ugandan money for

Kenyan. Jimmy had befriended a local Ugandan on the bus. Luckily, he kept us from getting ripped off. We constantly smiled and patted the African man on the back, our attempt to convince everyone that we were not strangers, nor alone. The man ate it up, laughing, smiling and putting his arm around us.

Outside the West, most people have no concept of a line. When people want something, they just push their way to the front. So there we were in a large crowd in Africa at midnight, holding our luggage, our money in our pockets, being bumped and pushed. Every money changer begged us to deal with him rather than the man beside him. I didn't speak unless I had to and did all I could to appear smooth and collected, as if I had changed my money there a hundred times.

We purchased our visas, pasted them into our passports, and then walked about one hundred yards into Kenya. Guards stood on the highway, holding rifles, stopping us to look at our papers. No gates were in sight. Anyone who truly wanted to evade the police and enter Kenya illegally could have easily done so simply by stepping off the road and trekking through the woods.

Once we stepped into Kenya, the buses pulled in behind us. We re-entered them and made our way to Nairobi, arriving just before sunrise. After three hours of standing and waiting with our luggage at the Nairobi bus station, a car approached us with a Kenyan driver. "Are you guys here for Made in the Streets?" he asked.

"Yes."

"I'm Philip. Jump in."

Jimmy started toward him, eager to see our trip to its end.

"Wait," I said, blocking him with my arm. "What are the supervisors' names?" I didn't trust anyone I didn't know.

"William and Jacey Colburn," he said, with a stunned expression.

"And what are our names?"

"Jimmy and Clayton."

And so, we began the next journey.

Chapter 8

We journeyed twenty miles out of Nairobi to the farm in the countryside. A baby-blue sky greeted us with clouds like cotton balls, stitched together and lengthened into feathered ends. We were taken to the boys' center: a dormitory and kitchen. The farm as a whole was a community of cement block homes surrounded by fields of bright green corn and knee-high savanna grass. The grassy fields stretched onward until they met the bottom of the blue-tinted mountains. There, staff claimed lions and anacondas still lived.

A vegetable garden with dark, rich soil and various greens, bursting forth from rows, lay protected by a barbed-wire fence. A cow with a bell dangling from its neck roamed the yards, and a fenced-in chicken coop with a rooster and hens sat at the back gates.

The supervisors of the farm were local Kenyans; some were staff from the local churches, while others were former street kids who had graduated from the program. That provided big brother/big sister relationships and mentoring, where the staff could assure the kids, "You can do it. Hang in there. We did."

At the farm, the kids could go to school, learn how to grow spinach, corn, cabbage, and collard greens, bake bread, care for goats, cows, and chickens, wash their own clothes and prepare their own meals. I lived in the boys' center on the farm, where I slept in a small apartment on the second floor of a three-story building. The boys' and girls' centers were separate, having their own dorms, kitchens, and bathrooms. Each center was gated off, with watchdogs protecting the living quarters. I had a private balcony at my apartment, where I could look out at the prairies and cornfields, which spread until they reached the mountains, colored blue from their distance.

I'm staying on a farm surrounded by hay and cornfields guarded by a worn wooden fence, covered with green ivy and red blossoms. It's like a picture in an Emerson poem. When I close my eyes, the smell of the hay takes me back home momentarily. Then, I am interrupted by children laughing and shouting words in Swahili. A pink sunset and a cool breeze brushing through the corn stalks and banana trees reminds me that I'm in another world. We just left the field where we raked hay and loaded it onto a trailer hooked to a farm tractor. I prepare this letter while sitting on my balcony, watching some of the former street kids lying on mounds of hay, talking, laughing and watching the corn stalks sway in the wind.

—Journal

Supporters of the program built a strip mall at the edge of the farm, near the highway that led into Nairobi. When the students turned seventeen, they were placed in job-skills training. The students could sell their carpentry work in the mall. Next door was the salon where the students trained as barbers. They even cut hair for people in the neighborhood at a discounted price. At the café, students were trained to be cooks. Travelers passing through could stop for breakfast and lunch. Each meal consisted of fresh vegetables from the farm and meat from the farmer's market.

I taught the English classes, while Jimmy spent most of his time in the Eastleigh slum interviewing street kids who met the criteria to come to the farm.

Our classes began at nine o'clock, meeting every hour with ten-minute recesses in between. We ate lunch together in the main kitchen located in the girls' center: beans, bread, cornmeal, eggs, and a green vegetable called *oogali*, which resembled turnip greens. When we entered the kitchen, bowls filled with the fresh cooked vegetables sat in rows on the table for students and staff. After the prayer, we took our bowls and ate. Though flies would cover the food, no one bothered to shoo them away. After having worked that morning in the fields or in the classroom, and with the aroma of the vegetables boiled in coriander, cumin, and cinnamon spices, you didn't care about flies.

The vegetable garden and cornfield, where the kids worked every afternoon, were planted in the boys' center. The kids pruned the crops, hoed the garden, fertilized the soil, picked and shucked corn and raked the hay for the cow that roamed the backyard. Then at three o'clock, the kids had free time on the full-length concrete basketball court with moveable soccer nets.

Near sundown, as students made their way back to their dorms, I joined the boys at our center, where we prepared dinner in the community kitchen: scrambled eggs mixed with greens and cornmeal, all cooked by boys thirteen and fourteen years old. I sat around the fire with them and listened to their conversations with each other in Swahili. When night fell and the moon and stars appeared, the boys picked fresh ears of corn and roasted it over the open flame as a late night snack. Cricket and locust songs rattled through the fields. Stars and their constellations, clearer in visibility than at the farm in Tennessee, covered the night sky.

I watched them drop creamed beans in the dirt by the fire and pick them back up and eat them without even blowing off the dust. They were used to it, due to living on the streets. When their conversations grew excited and their eyes were bright, I would ask one of the older boys what they were saying.

"They are talking about their former life on the streets," he would reply, or, "Just about something that happened today. One of the boys saw a rabbit and tried to catch it."

Though I could not decipher what was said, based on their facial expressions, laughter, hand motions, and my having come to know each of them individually, I almost understood their words.

Once, all the boys were adding to the conversation with laughter, their eyes wide and their hands gesturing. One of the supervisors told me, "Once when they were on the streets, all the boys from their base went out and begged for money and then came back and put all their money together in one lot. With that money, they went out and ate dinner at a restaurant and then went to a cinema and watched a movie together." It was the only life they knew. The streets were their past and they were remembering the good times, the freedom, and the relying on one another for survival.

They would ask me questions about the States: Do you have the moon and the stars there? Is it true wolves surround houses and break in and eat the people? I heard the actor from Superman died by getting stoned and jumping off a building, forgetting he was just an actor. Is that true?

I laughed, while turning my roasted corn over on the hot fire rocks. I would nibble at the cob when it was finished and tried my best to clarify their misconceptions. I enjoyed their company, their stories, and their questions. I was remembering their names, and they were remembering mine. They leaned back on their elbows and pointed at each other and laughed, recalling funny happenings on the streets. If they had spoken English and were raised in Tennessee, I wouldn't have been able to distinguish them apart from the boys I grew up with.

One night in particular, MITS received a new boy named Ken to the program. He spent the first two days walking around after every meal, eating the leftovers on everyone's plate because he wasn't sure if this whole three-meals-a-day thing would last. When they served chai tea, his eyes widened. "Chai tea! Do you know how much this costs? This is the rich man's tea!" The more wealthy Kenyans were known to drink it. A cup cost less than twenty cents in American currency.

That night by the fire, all the boys were laughing, talking, and making jokes. One of the sixteen-year-old boys looked at Ken and called him a black American. It was late, their stomachs were full and they were just being silly. They didn't mean to be insulting, but Ken took it as such. The poor kid burst into tears and walked about five steps away from the group, trying to gather himself.

One of the staff told Ken the kids were just playing. The other kids didn't scold or taunt him. Instead, they apologized. I wanted to walk over and hug the poor kid. I tried to improve the mood by telling Ken he could call me a white Kenyan. Everyone laughed, and Ken lightened up a bit. I had already told them before that if they forgot my name, they could call me Brother Vanilla.

I ventured into Eastleigh's city center every Monday and Wednesday. The air was filled with odors of rotting garbage and open sewage. We visited with the kids still living on the streets. Their ages ranged anywhere from twelve to eighteen. Some were abandoned by their parents, or their parents had died from diseases. Some of the parents couldn't afford to take care of their kids, so the kids tried to survive on their own.

Our custom, while visiting the street kids at their bases, was to purchase a meal of chapatti (flour fried in oil), beans, and potatoes for the kids, and talk with them throughout the afternoon. The restaurants in the slums were dirt pits surrounded by tin walls with a tin roof, and the food was cooked in an iron pot over an open fire. Though Eastleigh was known as the most dangerous slum in Nairobi, never once did I feel I was in danger during my stay.

"But never be in Nairobi after sundown," William warned. "Don't be foolish. Remember what happened."

Every street kid in Eastleigh knew about MITS. News traveled fast in that part of the city. But the addictive glue-sniffing and the free life on the streets were oftentimes just too alluring for them. Some wanted to return to the streets after they moved to the farm. A few new kids occasionally did run away, returning to the only life they knew. But there was a tremendous difference between the new kids and those who had been in the program even for just a year.

The kids on the farm acted like your average teenagers, while those who had just arrived were rowdy and ill-mannered, more like an eight-year-old boy who never had anyone to watch over or discipline him. There on the farm, living with the thirteen- to seventeen-year-olds, I often found Jimmy with tears in his eyes because it was clear how successful the program was in helping the kids.

When a kid moved into the streets, he sought a base. The kid was given permission to live there from the master (the oldest and strongest, proven by fighting).

Whatever money or food is given to the kids, they brought it back to the base and shared it. If a girl wanted to join, she had to sleep with the master and any of the other boys who desired her. She gave them sex, and they in turn provided her provisions and protection.

If the girls became pregnant, they could get an abortion from one of the women in the slum, costing about twenty shillings (seventy shillings equaled one American dollar). Not surgery, but a concoction, a drink. Other times, the girls had the baby, placed it in a plastic bag, and threw it in a dumpster. Some of the staff said that eight to ten babies were once found in a dumpster. Most were already dead.

Since the kids often went without food, they sniffed glue mixed with gas to numb their senses and dull their hunger pains. The kids also drank a beer called Changha (ten shillings a glass). One of the ingredients was water from the streets, contaminated with sewage, battery acid, and jet fuel.

Every Monday, the street kids came to the city center for a warm meal, a shower and a haircut. If we didn't shave their heads at the center, the kids did it with broken bottles on the street. At the gate of the center, the staff members would pat the kids down and take away their glue, which often led to the kids breaking down in tears.

In Eastleigh, since there are no police; the community was the police. If someone was caught stealing, a mob was formed and they placed a tire around the guilty party, poured gasoline on him, and set the thief on fire. The mob never doused the entire body in gasoline, for it was meant to punish rather than kill. Jimmy showed me pictures on his camera when he went into Eastleigh and photographed a man who was recently burned for stealing. Then, when the flames were put out, the mob discovered the thief was someone else.

Jimmy's photo showed the man sitting in nothing but shorts. White splotches dotted his right side as if someone took a paintbrush with white paint and tapped him down his body. The middle of the white markings had red, bloody centers. "I could tell that just moving his body hurt him," Jimmy said.

A girl at the farm, fifteen years old or so, asked me during class if I agreed with the burning of thieves.

"A man was burned by the mob because he stole," I told her.

"Yes."

"You think that person deserves to be burned?" I asked.

"Yes," she replied confidently. "Because he knew it was wrong."

Her response didn't surprise me. She was raised in the streets and it's all she knew before coming to the farm.

"So he was burned because he did something he knew was wrong?" I said.

"Yes."

"Have you ever done something you knew was wrong?"

She pressed her lips together and looked away.

"What if he stole bread to feed his starving children?" I continued. "Do you think we should burn him for that?"

She bit her lip and shook her head.

"You know," I said, "there is a quote from Jesus I like. He said, 'Blessed are the merciful for they will be shown mercy from God.' "

Saturday night was movie night. The kids gathered in one of the classrooms where William had set up a projector and DVD player, which he had recently purchased. I sat among the kids and some of the younger boys would cuddle up beside me and lay their heads against my shoulder.

I told Jimmy when we first arrived that, since most of those young boys were orphans by poverty, or because their families were murdered, and since they were beaten on the streets by older boys and shop owners, we should be intentional in hugging the new ones. Some new boys arrived at the farm during our second week. There were five boys, close friends, probably from the same base, all twelve to thirteen years old.

A street kid must be at least thirteen years old to come to the farm because Kenyan law required the younger ones to be sent to an orphanage. But there were no birth certificates, so a dentist estimated ages by examining the developmental stages of their teeth.

When I first raised my arms to hug them, one of the boys flinched, ready to dodge my fist. But I took his shoulders and pulled him into my arms, pressing his head against my chest. When I let go, his eyes had widened. Yet, by the end of the week, there he and the others were, huddling next to me in the movie room. They were slowly beginning to believe that the farm was safe after all.

After the movie, when I said goodnight to the boys, I escaped to my apartment for solitude. One of the African supervisors turned on the generator so Jimmy and I could have warm showers. Then I closed the day listening to music and writing in my journal.

I wrote about lots of things: life lessons I was learning, ideas for future economic development plans and experiences with the kids that were enlightening me. I thought about Tennessee and my family. I wrote them letters and called home every month during visits to the city center.

I also thought about Eden, reliving our conversations and time together, trying to put my finger on the times in our relationship where I could have been a better person. I reread the portions of my journal that detailed our time together, trying to relive each of our conversations in the cafés, at the beach and in my apartment, searching for clues that could help me understand why she may have left. But I found nothing.

On some nights, resentment and bitterness filled my heart, and I wanted to tear apart everything in my room.

I wondered if she ever thought about me, if she had regrets, if the events and circumstances that took her home had been resolved. Perhaps she did want to return but didn't know how. Maybe she did love me after all but was too afraid I would reject her or throw a fit of rage upon seeing her again. Then I would fall asleep holding my journal, while the music softly played and the candles burned in the background. I would wake in the morning and feel as if I was hungover, exhausted from emotion.

I pulled out a Bible Grandpa had given me before I left, and opened it to Matthew 13:44, where I kept a picture of me and Eden. I took that photograph during our night together on Valentine's Day. It was the only picture I had of us. She stood close to me, while I held the camera at arm's length. We had taken three or four photographs because either the camera wasn't at a good angle or Eden didn't like the way she looked in the photos. "Take it again," she said. "That one was bad of me."

"Well, I think you're pretty in all of them."

She huffed and smiled, shooing away my flattery. I took another, she was pleased with it, and I set the camera down. I cupped the back of her head with my hand and drew her to me once more, kissing her forehead. I remember her eyes were closed, and she smiled.

I held the photograph in my hands. Her head leaned into my cheek and her smile reassured me of our love. Though she left, at least she knew she was loved, I thought. I lay on my back and stared at her. I ran my fingers over her features, and then I examined the cheerful face of the boy who had no idea what Eden was about to do. Why didn't you stay away from her? I told him. Why couldn't you have obeyed your instincts and remained single? Then I placed the photograph back into my Bible and fell asleep.

One time, I took a three-hour bus into Nairobi and called Ryan, Joanna, and even Eden's professors, asking them if they knew anything. Nothing. So, I decided against my better judgement, and though Eden asked me not to contact her, I wrote her a handful of letters to her address in Colorado. I told her I still loved her, and that if she would just tell me what happened, I would still love her, and I could finally move on. Put closure on the past.

But she never responded.

I did everything imaginable to burn her out of my mind. I wrote down every memory of her, searching in hindsight for answers as to why she left. But I found nothing. I wrote our entire story, hoping it would bring peace and rest to my soul. But instead, I grew irritable and distrusting of people.

A year passed, but I remained in Africa. Though I grew closer to the community, I grew more desperate in the sort of loneliness that only a lover can fill. And the holes that a lost love leaves, I tried to fill with Taylor Blackwell. Taylor had graduated in international relations from Arizona State where she ran track. Now, she was teaching English in Tanzania through the AmeriCorps. She had emerald eyes, chestnut hair, and was just gorgeous.

A group of film and television majors from Pepperdine formed a student news crew, and were visiting the farm for two weeks to report on the street children's rehab program. Taylor was friends with one of the girls and agreed to meet up with her during her summer break. Taylor and I fell for each other quickly and hard. And we spent almost every day together for two months.

On Saturdays, we snuck away to a creek on the hillside that overlooked a game park. Giraffes, zebras, and sleepy lions roamed in the far distance, enclosed by fences. Taylor was my attempt to feel something again and to temper the sting of loneliness. She, too, missed the affections of former loves.

We lay on a blanket in the sage grass after a picnic. After lying in my arms, she adjusted her shirt and hair, and began to cover the baskets and plates. "You want to go into Nairobi this week-end, to the Java House?" she said over her shoulder.

"I have meetings." I refilled my glass with the half-empty bottle of whiskey at my side.

"Some teachers are going white-water rafting on the Nile next week. You want to go?"

"I've already done it," I answered. "Maybe next time."

"Maybe we can go to Kilimanjaro."

"No," I said, curtly.

"Well, I was just asking." When she returned to lie back down, her eyes lingered on my glass. "You know, that's your second bottle this week." I didn't even respond. Half my mind was else-where. On someone I knew a year ago. I took another drink. "What will happen when we leave Africa?" she asked.

"What do you mean?" I said, knowing full well what she meant.

"To us?"

"I'll go to Vanderbilt."

"What about me?"

She and I had had that conversation two or three times already. And I had been honest with her from the beginning, telling her the same thing over and over. But for some reason, she hung on.

"I can't, Taylor. And I've told you that. I have nothing left to give. I'm done. Okay?"

She pulled away and bit a trembling lip. A tear spilled out of her eye.

Taylor left Kenya a week later. We exchanged a letter or two over the years. But eventually that ended, too. Last I heard, she was married to a man who works in D.C., and they live in Maryland.

There's a video of Taylor and I on Pepperdine's Project Serve website. The news crew had interviewed William, myself, and some of the other staff members. And in one of their b-rolls of the farm, I'm leaving the news set with my back to the camera. Taylor runs over to me, takes my hand in hers, and kisses my cheek. I hang my arm around her and we walk off camera together.

I haven't seen that video in years, but I haven't forgotten it. She was a lovely girl with a good heart. And I'll be forever sorry for whatever pain I caused her.

PART III

PART III

Eden switched on the lamp, illuminating her living room. She set Finn's book aside and closed the blinds on her sliding glass window. She stepped into the kitchen and riffled through her mail as she rang her dad. She lifted a colored postcard from Pepperdine, advertising their Homecoming that coming weekend.

"Hey, sweetie," her dad answered.

"Hi, Dad. One of my friends said he sent me some letters some years back. Letters from Africa."

"Africa?" he responded, surprised.

"Yeah. Do you ever remember that?"

"No, I'm sorry, honey," he said. "Your mother checked the mail and forwarded you everything. But you know her memory was bad."

"There's a reunion at Pepperdine this weekend."

"Yeah."

"I think I might go. If I do, I'll come by the house on my way."

"That would be great, honey! Come back by on your way home from Pepperdine, too. I'd love to see you again. I miss you."

"I miss you, too. And I will, if I go."

"Okay. I hope so."

"Okay."

Eden ended the call and sunk back down into the couch. She lifted Finn's book again, and read.

Chapter 9

Another year passed. And with time, the light cast from the street children's love for us, our love for them, the community we shared with each other, my friendship with the staff, and the children's need for our continual attention and care, helped me feel at home in Africa. I found myself smiling more, and once, following an off-hand remark from one of the kids, I recall laughing so hard my chest hurt. So, as Grandpa predicted, time did pass, and the ache of Eden's absence slowly faded into the shadows.

One evening, William and Jacey took Jimmy and me to a coffee shop in the expatriate side of Nairobi where buildings, hotels and streets were clean and maintained. From there, I called Ryan and Oz and shared the happenings in Eastleigh. Oz had told me once, while we were at Pepperdine, that he wanted to be a part of something meaningful. So we talked through some ideas, and he set up an account to send fifteen dollars a week so we could purchase daily water, corn, avocados and multivitamins for all the kids.

Oz solicited monetary support from an uncle who owned a martial arts dojo, and a lot of the fighters contributed as well. William and Jacey were then able to open the city center every day so the kids could receive a warm, healthy meal. William must have thanked me a hundred times for it. But we weren't finished. This was meant to only sustain the kids while we set up a micro-lending institution.

One of the street kids, Solomon, grew up in a home where his mother owned a sewing machine and made shirts and trousers for people in the community. She even had a contract to make school uniforms for the local school district. When his mother was killed during the massacre, though Solomon had been taught how to sew clothes, he was young and inexperienced and sold the sewing machine for less than half its worth. He said he had to provide food for himself and his two younger brothers.

So we decided to do something about it. The same street kids always showed up at the city center for the meals. Therefore, over time, we became their friends and trusted caretakers. So we pulled aside four kids whom we recognized as leaders among their peers, along with Solomon, and we made them a deal. They were to elect a single leader among themselves. We would give this leader fifteen dollars to purchase a sewing machine and enough cloth and thread to produce three shirts.

If, over the course of fourteen weeks, they repaid us one dollar each week, they would qualify for a much larger loan to purchase more sewing machines and cloth. But they wouldn't get another loan until the previous loan was paid in full. We told them that they must work together to back their elected leader, so that he wouldn't fail, and ruin the chances of their team receiving a larger loan. The kids were also told that the money they returned would then be loaned to other poor people so they could feed their families. So not only were the kids receiving money for themselves, but they were giving back to their community, and helping rescue each other out of severe poverty.

The plan worked.

Solomon made three very colorful shirts of bright yellow, purple and brown, with tribal-style designs. The five boys worked together and sold two of them in the marketplace. Of course, if they hadn't sold them, we knew more than enough people in the States who were willing to buy the shirts. Oz asked for the third shirt, which he purchased and hung in Mike's dojo as a reminder of what microlending can do for third-world communities.

We made the boys a deal, so when the amount was paid back in full, we tripled the loan, and within a month, they were operating a full-time sewing business. I learned the concept of microlending through Hope International, and passed it along to William and Jacey. Years have passed now, and there have been numerous microloans

microloans awarded to not only the street kids, but poor parents who were elected as the leaders of their community to receive the loan.

The success rate has been ninety-eight percent. Those that failed were due to things like the loan being spent on a medical bill to save a family member's life. Traditionally, since the elders of the village vouch for and decide which business savvy member receives the loan, the loan is forgiven and a new one issued.

Not long after the microlending success, I was eating lunch at the farm when Simon, the mailman, handed me a letter, addressed from my dad.

Dear Clayton,

Your Granddaddy always asks when you're coming home. He's much older now, and frail. He fell, not long ago, and has trouble getting around. He also gets sick often, and I'm afraid he won't be with us much longer. Your mother and I miss you and we all wish you would come home as soon as possible. I love you, Dad.

So after spending five years at the farm in Nairobi, I announced that I would be returning home.

Chapter 10

During my last night in Kenya, the kids invited me to the Saturday night movie. While we sat on the park benches, our backs leaning against the wall and my arms around them, it was hard for me to decide where I wanted to be. I wanted to be that older brother to the kids but my custom was to spend my Saturday nights on walks under the moon and stars with the staff members. Our walk always concluded with dinner together. We cooked our food over an open fire, and then we sat and ate together and talked.

So I stayed with the kids through half the movie and then I joined the staff members for dinner in Philip's dorm. Philip, Chance, and Moses were staff I had grown to know and call close friends, and they welcomed me with smiles and handshakes. Philip handed me a plate of oogali and cornmeal, and I sat down on one of the stools.

"So, this is your last night, yes?" Chance asked.

"Yes."

"And your time here was good, yes?"

"Yes. It was."

"When you first came here to us, you were very quiet," Moses added. "But over time, you came to be smiling and laughing. Now, these days, you have become quiet again. Is Clayton's heart sad?"

I looked across the room and all the guys were waiting for an answer. "When I first came here, there was a lot I needed to figure out about myself. I believe I did find conclusions. But I also know that when I return to my home in Tennessee, things I have ignored will be awaiting me."

"Mmmm," they said, nodding their heads.

"Your family misses you, yes?" asked Chance.

"Yes. And I miss them."

"No woman back home?" Moses asked.

"No," I said, shaking my head, pretending the subject was as trivial as the weather.

"Well, we are glad you came. Africa will miss you. You will come back, yes?"

"Perhaps one day," I said. Then we settled into a conversation about our times together.

"Don't forget Clayton is leaving this evening. So make sure you say goodbye to him," William announced the next morning during breakfast. The staff smiled and nodded their heads. Most of the kids glanced at me briefly, and then looked down at the ground, or away. William walked over to me. "Clayton, we got a call about thirty minutes ago from the embassy. They said you need to report to their office before you leave the country."

"Is that normal?"

"No, but I wouldn't be worried. It's probably something about your length of time here or about your passport."

"Did they give a time that they wanted me to come by?"

"No, and that's why I don't think there's a problem. But if they called here, it's important."

"Okay. I'll take a matatu into the city." William thought that was a good idea, so I took the staff members Moses and Chance with me. When we arrived to the embassy, men in navy-blue uniforms and white gloves guarded the entrances with assault rifles. They asked to see my passport, which I showed them, and they allowed the three of us to enter the lobby.

The walls, a crème sheetrock, were decorated with framed photos of Washington, D.C. and Langley. Glossy, white tile floors reflected people's shoes and trousers as they walked. Ceiling fans stuttered, trying to chase out the humidity. A handful of Africans waited in the lobby, sitting in blue plastic chairs in a large square formation, like something you would see in a doctor's office. I signed in at the front desk and sat with Moses and Chance.

A woman in jeans and a t-shirt came out of a door beside the front desk. Multiple ID tags hung from her neck and she carried herself with authority. I could see past her and through the hallway, into a labyrinth of cubicles and offices.

Her expressionless face bothered me. She seemed bored and apathetic. "Clayton Fincannon," she said, looking right at me. I rose and she smiled a diplomatic smile. When I passed, she closed the door behind us, and led me into an office a few yards down the hall and to the right.

Behind a finished wooden desk sat a barrel-chested African-American man in jeans and a gray t-shirt with a Marine Corp logo. He stood, smiled, and extended his hand. He couldn't have been older than thirty. On his desk sat a wooden plaque with a black, marble front, engraved with the words, *James Duncan*. Business cards with the same military logo sat beside the plaque. "Gunnery Sergeant Duncan," he said.

"Clayton Fincannon," I replied, shaking his hand.

"Grab a seat, young man."

I sat in a foldable, gray, metal chair, and he sat behind his desk in a leather swivel one. His demeanor was calm, his fingers interlocked, and he rested his hands in his lap. I mimicked him by leaning back and interlocking my fingers, too. He rocked back and forth in his chair, examining my expression.

"Let me just go ahead and tell you, you're not in trouble," he said.

"Okay. Where are you from?" I hoped to make the climate a bit more relaxed and personal. I also wanted to remind him that we were from the same nation, and both visitors in this country.

He must have known this was my last day, or else the embassy wouldn't have called.

He chuckled and relaxed his shoulders. I hadn't realized they were tense. "I'm from Arizona," he said.

"I'm from Tennessee."

"Yes, I know." We smiled at each other. "We saw in our system all the places you've traveled. And you've been here five years working with street kids."

"Yes, sir."

"You have stamps from all over the world. Spain. Gibraltar. Morocco. Romania. India. And the list goes on."

I spotted two or three pieces of paper stacked on his desk. They were travel articles I had written. I knew because my picture was on them. He must have printed them directly from the Internet. He lifted a single printed page from under his keypad. He held it in front of him, briefly looking it over, as if refreshing his memory. "It says you received some training under a Major John Jacobson while you were in North Africa. A Marine Corp man."

"Yes, sir."

"Tell me about that."

"About Major Jacobson or the training?"

"Both," he said, with an inquisitive smile, his eyes locked on mine. I didn't know if he was fishing for something, or toying with me. Either way, it seemed he knew something I didn't, or he wanted me to believe he did.

"We were working with street orphans, and Major Jacobson trained us in areas so that if we ever got in trouble, we could flee the country. He was a major for a while, but he's not in the military anymore."

"What kind of trouble?"

"Well, it's not popular to be Christian there. And if you're white and from the west, they believe you're Christian. Even if just nominally. If they accused us of being missionaries, they could arrest us. So he was teaching us stuff we could use at that time and for the future. He was a teacher. I learned a lot from him."

Gunnery Sergeant Duncan nodded and returned his eyes to the document. "It says here that you learned star navigation, anti-terrorism training, self-defense, desert hygiene, water extraction from trees and even courses on Arabic and Islam."

"Yes, sir."

"Why all of that?"

"Major Jacobson had served as a high school teacher for a while. That's one of the reasons why he was leading the team. But he also wanted to teach us military tactics just in case we might need them in the future. He had trained soldiers for years. I think it was his way of continually giving back."

The sergeant nodded. Then he leaned forward

in his chair and rested his elbows on his desk. His smile disappeared. "The reason I ask is, we're partnering with the U.N. in forming a mercenary team to track down Joseph Kony and his rebels." The sergeant then set the paper back on the desk and resumed rocking back and forth again. "Do you know who Kony is?"

"Yes, sir."

"Okay. The problem is, we have to earn the trust of the locals in the villages. They'll help us locate him. We can't send in Africans because the people in the villages don't trust other Africans. They don't know if they're spies or not. But they trust foreigners because they know we aren't emotionally attached to the war. We need some people to be good public relationists, to go out with the U.N., build relationships with villagers. In those areas, they'll know where Kony is hiding, and help us find him. Then, we'll send in a special team to hunt him down."

"Don't you have guys who are trained to meet with locals and scout out those things?" I asked.

"With Liberia, Libya, Sierra Leone, Somalia and Sudan, and everything else that's going on in Africa, there's little help. Besides, with you being here five years, and the training you've had, you're probably more qualified that anyone I could get. You're from Tennessee, too. You probably know how to handle a gun, right? And have good aim?"

"Yes, sir, but I'm not going to use one."

"No, we wouldn't ask that. But you might have to pick one up."

"Look," I said, shuffling to the edge of my seat. "They were deer rifles and shot guns. Pellet guns, when I was a child. They weren't AK-47s."

"What I'm saying is, you have some experience. We don't expect you to use a gun. But if you ever did, you wouldn't need much training in it."

"What if I say no?"

"Then you say no, and you go home."

"So what's needed of me?" I wasn't planning on staying, but I wanted to get a thorough understanding of what the situation was.

"We need you to be part of the team that goes out and has the conversations with the locals, the villagers. We'll have translators for you. You'd have a phone that you'd use to call our base in Kampala. You'd brief us daily on how things are going. And when we find out where Kony is, your job's done."

I sat forward on my elbows and rubbed my eyes. I slid my hands across the sides of my head and gripped the back of my neck. I might have sat like that for a few seconds, but I finally let my chin rest in my palms. "Gunnery Sergeant, I've been here five years. It was supposed to be just for one summer. My grandfather's sick. And I want to go home."

"Every Christmas, do you know what Kony

does? He celebrates it by reminding Uganda that he's still around. He enters the northern villages, and chops off hands and noses, showing off his power. That's how rebels believe they win respect, by creating terror, fear."

"So, you want me to go into northern Uganda?"

"No, that's not where he is. He's hiding in Congo. That's where you'll go. You'll be visiting villages and tribes who don't have much connection with the outside world. Some of them have never seen a white man before. They've heard about white people, but they've never seen them. White people have a good reputation in these parts of Africa, because the only white people who come here are humanitarians and missionaries. The best schools in Africa can be traced back to the work of missionaries. And back then, they were all white."

I sat back in my chair and looked up at the ceiling. I couldn't get mad at the sergeant for asking me to stay. He was just doing his job. The embassy wouldn't have called me if they didn't feel it was necessary. I shot out of my chair, sending it crashing into the wall. Echoes of fingers typing on keypads in cubicles across the hall stopped. The air was still for a moment, and then papers began shuffling again and typing resumed. I didn't look over at the sergeant. I wasn't too concerned about his reaction, anyway.

Internally, I was shaking my head. I almost

started crying right there in his office. I didn't want to stay. And though I knew my conscience might bother me for years to come, I made my decision.

I walked to the door, turned back to face him, and leaned against the doorjamb. I put my hands in my front jeans' pockets and relaxed my weight on one foot. "I've been here five years," I stated again. "It's time I go home."

Gunnery Sergeant nodded, accepting my decision. Then he stood and took a business card from his desk and handed it to me. "If you get home and change your mind, contact me. My email and number's on there, okay?" I nodded, took his card, and left. When I opened the door into the lobby, Moses and Chance stood with expectant faces. I nodded at them and motioned toward the exit.

"What happened?" Moses asked, standing the closest to me. Chance sped to my other side, hoping to hear my answer as we left the embassy together.

"They just wanted me to stay in Kenya longer," I said.

"Will you?" Moses asked.

"No. I can't."

When we returned to the farm, William asked if everything was okay. I told him, and everyone else who asked, the same reply I had given Moses.

"The embassy wanted me to stay longer and help, but I said no."

That evening, I helped Joel, one of the supervisors, prepare some hot chocolate at the boys' center, trying to forget my meeting with the sergeant. Every Friday evening at five o'clock, the boys gathered under the pavilion for an activity called Cell Group where Joel led them in songs. Then they sat in a circle and talked about the past and present, like group therapy. One of the newer boys, Simon, was the sharpest kid in my English class. But he was struggling with the idea of returning to the streets because his family sent word that they missed him.

I pulled Simon aside after the session. "Always ask yourself, 'Whatever decision I make, ten years from now, will I be grateful for that decision or will I regret it?' You're a leader now, you're a sweet kid, and you're one of the smartest kids here. One day, you will lead these boys. I know that. And I know it's hard here. But you hang in there. You don't want to go back to the streets. You've been there. You know where all that ends." I had seen it myself. So had Simon. Twenty-year-olds, having been raised on the streets, waddling and stumbling down the road because their brains were fried from sniffing glue.

Simon placed his hands together as if to pray, and then bowed to me. I saw a picture of him some years later. He was seventeen and preparing to leave the farm as a graduate of the program. He planned to be a chef.

At the end of Cell Group, we passed out the cups of hot chocolate. The boys stood in a circle as I gave a farewell speech. I told them that when I arrived, the Kenyans never treated me as a stranger or teacher, but as family. And I felt like family. "If you are ever tempted to leave the farm and go back to the streets, remember that you have a family here who loves you. Don't miss that." Then in Swahili, I told them all that Jimmy and I loved them. Those words were followed with the kids and staff cheering and clapping and taking turns hugging us.

They all asked me if I would take their picture so I wouldn't forget them. "Will you write to us? Will you ever come back?" I answered yes to all of them, though half suspecting that over time, our memories of each other would fade and it would be as if I had never been there.

As we boarded the van for the airport, I walked over to William. "So this is it."

"The kids really connected with you. And I know they're sad to see you go. We wish you'd stay, but we know you have a life to live back home. Tell Ryan we said hello. Jacey is still at the market, so she'll miss saying goodbye. But listen, we'll be back at Pepperdine soon."

"Well, I finished my studies there."

"Oh," he said. "So what's next?"

"I don't know. My experiences, the life I have lived here, it's given me a lot to think about. Things I'll think about for a long time."

"I know it will, Clayton." I looked over at the truck and Joel was awaiting us. I reached out and hugged William.

"Clayton?" William said, when I turned to leave.

I paused and glanced back. "Yeah?"

"I love you," he said, looking into my eyes like a proud father.

I smiled like a thankful son. "I love you, too. Tell Jacey I said bye."

"I will," he said.

Chapter 11

When I arrived at the Nashville airport in October, I greeted Mom and Dad with long hugs. They didn't have many questions since they had received my letters. But when I tried to tell them other things that took place during those years, I felt a barrier between us. No matter what I expressed through song, poem, or story, comprised of the symbols we call words, neither they nor anyone else would truly understand all the things the people and experiences of East Africa taught me. So there I was, feeling alone again.

Back at the farm, Mom and Dad walked with me to Grandpa's house. A lot of the flowers that once adorned his property had withered away.

"Grandpa?" I yelled, playfully, hopping onto the porch.

"Now Clayton," Mom warned, "don't get upset."

Fear pulsated through my chest. Then Grandpa popped the screen door open with his crutch. "Clayton?" He limped out. He looked like he had aged ten years and his clothes looked two sizes too large. He stumbled, but grabbed the wall. We all ran to assist him. Then I led him to a rocking chair so he could rest.

"He fell in the spring," Mom said. "The doctors said he'd get better, but it's been a slow process."

"Oh, I'm fine.

"Tea, please?" he said, motioning to Dad. Dad and Mom both entered the house, I suppose, to give Grandpa and me a moment alone. Grandpa squeezed my shoulder. "Are you happy?"

"I am," I said, nodding and smiling. "You?"

Grandpa nodded and pulled me in for a tight hug. Mom and Dad returned with two Mason jars filled with sweet tea and lemons. I pulled out gifts from my bag. I gave Mom Masai bracelets made from red, white, green, and black beads.

"The lady who I bought that from can now feed her family for a month," I told her.

For Dad, I brought him a knife with a lion bone handle. And for Grandpa, a box of African tea which they used for milk-tea.

"You brew it with milk instead of water," I told him.

"He hasn't been able to work on the farm much," Dad said.

"Your mom's been a great help," Grandpa told me. "But she can't keep up the gardens."

"We hired gardeners but they never did the kind of job he liked," Mom added.

"I'll get this place back into shape," I said, squatting in front of him. "It'll be beautiful again, just like it once was."

"We'll work together!" he said grabbing my hand.

"You bet we will!"

I spent the next couple of months taking trips from the nursery to the farm, replanting all the flowers that once flourished. And I helped Dad with the cattle. Grandpa was in his late eighties by then, but still tried to work like a man in his forties. They piled limbs, while I dragged off fallen trees with the tractor and split and stacked the firewood.

In the beginning of December, I began cleaning out my chester drawers and sorting through boxes shipped home from Pepperdine five years prior. My phone rang while it was charging on the end table beside my bed. I lifted my phone and looked at the number. Local. I sat down on my bed. "Hello?"

"Mr. Fincannon?"

"Yes?"

"This is Dean Willis from Vanderbilt. I'm the department chair in the literature program."

"Yes, sir," I said, standing up.

"Dr. Daniels from Pepperdine called me last week. He had a copy of your transcripts and test scores sent over from the admissions department. He said you wouldn't mind. Are you still interested in pursuing a Ph.D.?"

"Yes, sir."

"Well, he told us about your work with the street kids in Kenya and that you came highly recommended. I knew Dr. Daniels at Princeton. He's a good man."

"Yes, sir, he is."

"Well, we had a faculty meeting this morning, and we'd like to offer you a position of adjunct professor here while you pursue your Ph.D. with us."

"Really? My Ph.D. will be fully covered?"

"It sure will. We'll provide you a free place to live in our graduate school apartments and we'll even award you with a stipend for your services as a professor."

For some reason, though I'm not sure why, I wasn't as excited as I should have been. A part of me didn't even care anymore. "Sounds good. Thank you. Where do we go from here?"

"We'll send you some documents to sign, and we'll see you next fall."

"Okay. Thank you."

I hung up the phone and continued shuffling through my things. My parents and Grandpa all knew that teaching and studying at Vanderbilt was a lifelong dream of mine, but I decided not to say anything until the documents arrived.

On my desk lay stacks of mail and books and notebooks from Pepperdine. In a box, I found the photograph Joanna took of me, Ryan, and Oz on the lacrosse field. And I found *A Severe Mercy*, the book Eden loved. When I lifted the book, Eden's hair tie fell out.

I remembered the day I kept her hair tie. We were lying on a blanket in the park, as was our custom. I had read a portion of the book to her, and a love scene had just ended in the story. Eden lifted her head from my chest, took the book, set it aside, and kissed me. I removed the tie from her hair, letting her dark strands fall into and around my face. I wrapped the hair tie around my wrist while we kissed.

Suddenly weak in my knees, I sat on my bed and drew a shaky breath.

After that night, more dreams of her followed. Some were true events from the past. And others were what could have been.

In one dream, we had ventured to our farm in Tennessee before visting her parents in Colorado. It was a lovely spring day where the sun and cool breeze made the world just right. All the trees and flowers bloomed and various orange, purple, and yellow butterflies filled the air. Pink flower petals fell from the sky as we rode horses in the pasture. I took her to Reedy Creek where I once played as a child. We tied the horses to a tree and walked along the brook.

"What happened to your grandmother?" she asked.

"She died before I was born. Granddaddy sold the paper to take care of her. When they were seventeen, she almost married someone else."

"What happened?"

"Grandpa climbed into her bedroom window and said he loved her."

"That's sweet," Eden said.

"It freaked out her parents."

Eden leaned back and laughed from her belly.

I stepped across the brook and helped her across. "She's the one who planted the flowers. So Granddaddy keeps them alive."

"He's wonderful."

"He is. Now close your eyes." I led her to a clearing where gushing water pounded on the rocks. "Open."

Her jaw dropped. The water emptied into a swimming hole. Birds flew and sang in the branches. Fish rolled in the water. And the pink petals still floated down around us.

"I use to swim here and lay under that tree. And promise myself that one day I'd save the world. Isn't that funny?"

Eden wrapped her arms around my neck. "I think you have an old soul."

"Yeah?"

"Yeah."

"Is that a good thing?" I asked.

"It's a very good thing. I'm going to start calling you Grandpa," she said, winking.

"You can," I replied, "when we have grand-children."

"And will you love me when I have wrinkles and gray hair?"

"I'll love you then, more than ever," I said. She kissed me, deeply.

Suddenly, we were in her parents' home in Colorado. Now, withered, darker petals fell. Her parents had just summoned her to the kitchen. When she found me later, she buried her face into my neck and cried. Dark, dead, crisp petals fell. Her crying wouldn't stop. The tears gushed, uncontrollable and inconsolable weeping, the tears growing larger and heavier. Then, her tears turned to great drops of blood. "FINN!" she screamed.

I woke.

I thought that by serving the children in Africa, I would find complete healing. However, experience taught me otherwise. No matter where you are, that's where you are. You take yourself with you. Over the years, I had fought and fought to keep from thinking about her. I kept pushing her out of my thoughts, replacing them with new street children projects, bettering old ones, establishing new friendships, reading, writing, praying and listening to music.

Back home, the farm work helped some but wasn't a cure-all. So I began spending my early mornings reading novels over coffee, trying to distract my mind by losing it in stories. I worked on the farm, and then I went to the gym to lift weights and swim. All of it soothed the burdensome feelings, but none of it stopped the inner turmoil. I couldn't get that dream or any of the others I had of her out of my mind.

When I wasn't working or trying my best to occupy my thoughts with something other than her, she consumed me. Anything that hinted at femininity sent images and memories of her charging through my thoughts. I couldn't shake them away, no matter how hard I tried. Her mouth near mine, our words and kisses searching through and exploring their depths. Her wild, eager eyes, burning into my soul with their passion. Her strength, and the personal security with which she kissed me. Our long talks. Our congruous philosophies. Her scent on my pillow. And now, the pain and despair she was possibly experiencing.

I knew I could pick up the telephone and called her. I could write her again. But I refused. I was now afraid of why she left. I was afraid that my contacting her would make matters worst. What if she hated me for contacting her? There was a reason she didn't want me to follow. And she had asked that if I loved her, not to. I was also afraid of my reaction upon hearing her voice or seeing her face again. I was afraid I would fall harder for her and still be told no. I was afraid she would consider it melodramatic that I still believed I loved her.

So one morning, I knocked on Grandpa's door, to visit with him, but he was gone. So I pulled out a letter I wrote the night before and dropped it in the Mason jar.

Grandpa,

It has been over five years now, and Eden has still not left my thoughts. I'm almost thirty years old, and I wonder if I will ever want to love someone like that again. Even though years have passed and sometimes I feel that if she came back today, I would have to say no to her, there are days when I think of her and miss her so much that I would give away all my material possessions to spend a day with her and hold her again. Therein, a renewed love could exist between us and I could hold her on sunny and rainy afternoons while she sleeps, or while watching a movie, or at dinner with friends, or even on a couch at Christmas as we watch loved ones open gifts. I wonder if the melancholy will ever leave me.

There are times I miss her so incredibly that people ask me with concerned faces if I'm okay. I wish for days where I could hold her again with no words exchanged, and other days when I wish the memory of her would leave my life, days when I want to shake her shoulders and yell, "What's wrong with you?! You stupid, foolish, stubborn girl!" Then, as strange as it sounds, days follow when I'm content. I stand in the warm sunshine as my mind dwells on the goodness of humanity, and I think of her and my past with warm sentiment and a thankful heart.

I am trying to make sense of the situation and what God wants with me, but nothing is forthcoming. God is silent. Absent. All I find from Him is a slammed door. If I had said or done something to deserve her leaving, I would understand. Then, I could have offered an apology to at least stay on speaking terms and continue a friendship. However, based on everything I know and remember, she left due to no fault of mine.

When you love family members and friends and they leave to return to their homes or to move into a new town, they will communicate through phone calls or letters. They know they are loved and they return that love. But if the person you love leaves and vanishes and leaves no clues . . . and you never know if they're happy or sad, or dead or alive; no one can describe the pain you feel, not even a poet. I wouldn't wish that kind of pain on anyone, not even my enemies. I am trying to make sense of something I cannot. Do you have any words for me, Grandpa?

I love you,

—Clayton

That evening, Grandpa called and said a fire was awaiting us in the fire pit on his back porch. We sat warming ourselves for three hours, talking. We drank from our Mason jars as I reflected on Africa. He mentioned the letter and began asking questions that prodded my heart, a subject I both longed for and dreaded. I wanted it all to be over, whether Eden and I were meant to be together or not. My soul and mind were spent, and I just wanted peace.

"Still no word?" he said.

I shook my head. I adjusted my coat against the chill and stared into the fire.

"I had another dream about her."

"Yeah?" Grandpa said, leaning toward me on his armrest, his chin resting in his hand.

"It was years from now, but we were still young. It was nighttime, and we were staying in a skyline hotel with a balcony that overlooked the city. We had just returned from a fundraiser of some sort. I was wearing a white dress-shirt with black slacks, and I was pulling off my black tie. She was dressed in a black skirt with black pantyhose and standing by the window with the lights from the skyscrapers behind her. She stepped out of her shoes and tilted her head to remove one of her diamond earrings. She was smiling at me with her radiant eyes, which I remember so vividly. I was thankful that I had married her. It was years later, and I was still very much in love with her."

"Let me tell you something I know from experience," Grandpa said. "One day you'll meet a woman whom you'll love more than Eden and that love will be reciprocated. When it happens, you'll thank God things didn't work out with Eden. You'll be reminded that God has the best in mind for us and He knows what He's doing. But I'll also tell you, Clayton, that if you want to find out how she is, you have that opportunity."

"What, you mean contact her?"

"Why not? It's been five years, and you haven't gotten over her. You don't have closure because you never found out what happened or why she disappeared, and how she feels now. You want to know how she's doing? And don't you think she'd probably like to hear what you've been up to?"

I nodded. "Maybe. I wish that were so."

"You probably could see her again if you really wanted to. Most people don't have that chance."

"A part of me hates her," I said, surprised at my admittance. I felt my heart thud against my chest.

"Well, a part of you will probably always love and hate her. She might want to know about you. But if she knows how badly she hurt you, wouldn't that keep her away?"

I watched the ambers crack, sending up bursts of little flames and sparks with the smoke. "You know what I'd like to know?"

"Hmm?"

"I'd like to know why she left, to hear her views in hindsight. I'd also like her to know how much I loved her, but also, how resentful I've been. Angry. I think if I knew exactly what happened and why, I could find closure."

"If she wants to get back together, would you take her back? You need to be able to answer that question before you see her again."

"I don't know what I'll do. But I agree. If anything's possible between us, if we can be together again, or if it's meant to be over and I move on, I need to know."

"I'd reach out to her. She might be glad to hear from you. Remember, you're a part of her past too."

"When you climbed into grandmother's room as a teenager," I said, "what if that had pushed her further away? And she had said no?"

"That didn't happen."

"But what if it did?"

"I would have known the truth."

"What?"

"That we weren't meant to be together. If she didn't love me, she would've said no."

At that, Grandpa stirred the fire, while I pondered the consequences of my next move.

I entered Grandpa's kitchen and took my cell phone from my pocket. I looked up Eden's phone number to her home in Colorado. I still had her cell number too, but had thought it wise not to call it. I called her parents. Mrs. Valmont, with a weak voice, answered the phone.

"Hello?"

"Mrs. Valmont? I'm an old friend of Eden's."

"Yes," she answered, amicably.

"I haven't seen her since college and I just wanted to check on her."

"She and her husband are doing fine. Their work keeps them busy."

I lost my strength and leaned against the wall. "Her husband?" I confirmed.

"Yes. And what was your name?"

I hung up the phone and heard the floor creak behind me. I turned to find Granpda standing in the kitchen.

"I'm sorry, son," he said.

I nodded and stepped out onto the back porch. Lightning bugs and the songs of the tree frogs filled the summer air.

Chapter 12

Growing up, I had the naïve notion that if I lived the right way, if I refrained from having dirty thoughts about girls or using foul language, if I kept my shirt tucked in and my hair combed, and never thought badly about anyone, I would be rewarded with the kind of life and wife I always wanted. We'd have a great marriage, a loving home, the dog we always wanted, and butterflies and honeybees would fly atop the plethora of flowers in our garden, year-round.

Adulthood was nothing like I imagined as a boy. Instead of dreams coming true, life was becoming more of a disappointment.

I missed the person I was before I met her. The boy who was so full of joy, who looked forward to tomorrow, who couldn't wait to roll out of bed and begin the day. I also missed my friends Ryan and Oz. And I missed Pepperdine. If I did take the offer from Vanderbilt, life would grow hectic again, and I wouldn't have time to spend with my friends. Ryan was married to Joanna and still working as an academic advisor at Pepperdine, Oz was graduating with his Doctorate in clinical psychology, so I flew to Pepperdine to visit and attend Oz's December graduation.

I hadn't seen Ryan since we parted in Uganda.

He had purchased some Cuban cigars during a trip to Canada and when we met up in California, he asked me to smoke one with him. And we invited Oz.

Ryan and I found a table outside Dietrich's coffee shop and Oz joined us for a short while. Oz's family had come to be with him for his graduation. They finished dinner at the Malibu Market and joined us for coffee. I told them stories about my experiences in Africa and Oz's family took turns sharing fond memories of his childhood. They visited with us for an hour or so, and then Oz took them to see some of the tourist attractions in Hollywood.

Ryan and I finally found ourselves alone, and I was reminded of the comfort and security I felt when I was near him. Ryan knew every bad thing I had ever done, yet he never treated me differently because of it. And I was the same way with him. I thank God for people like that.

The fountain spewed its water. Birds perched in the rafters and chirped lazily back and forth before drifting off to sleep. Ryan and I nursed our coffee and propped our feet on opposite chairs. The aroma of the freshly brewed coffee filled our noses. The night was chilly, so we wore our coats. Ryan lit his cigar and took a few puffs.

"Are you glad to be home, Finn?" His eyes told me he wasn't just making small talk.

"I am glad to be home. I'm glad to be here with

you, to see friends I haven't seen in ages. It's nice also, to be back in Tennessee. To have some home cooking and to sit with Mom and Dad and to see Grandpa again. I haven't been home long, so it's natural to keep reliving the African experiences over and over again. I do miss Africa. The kids, William and Jacey, the community we had, the food and the routines."

Ryan tapped his cigar with his forefinger, knocking off a block of ash. "And Eden?"

I loved Ryan like a brother, but I wasn't going to tell him everything. So I gave him a brief version of the story, that I had written her and she didn't respond, that I called her parents and she was married.

"You know," I said. "I honestly can't stand the idea of being with a woman anymore. It was nothing like I imagined as a boy. I really am considering just living my life as a professor and missionary, teaching and traveling alone. Caleb got married and his wife is like a sister to me. One day they'll have kids. I still have my parents and friends like you. You guys are family. Why should I begin my own when I'm already blessed with so much?"

"Wow, Finn." Ryan said with a raised brow. "Look, I know you've been hurt. I have too. But the life of celibacy must be chosen out of joy, not sadness, and not because you've been hurt by a woman. I shut down from women for a few years and then I talked to one of my mentors. He helped me realize I've been cynical of women, not because of the women, but because of the stuff that took place within me, my reaction to what they did. It's not what people do, but it's our reaction to it."

"I understand that, but I just don't want to do it anymore. All the dressing up and all the chasing each other, the sexes battling and using each other and trying to impress each other, it all seems so vain."

"You were single all the way up to the time you met Eden. Do you realize that in your thirty years of life, you've only been with one woman? And you already want to throw in the towel because it didn't work out?"

I thought that was a bit of an understatement. It wasn't just that it didn't work out. She vanished. But still, after hearing his words, I wondered if I was being ridiculous.

"Listen," he continued. "The reason women get dressed up and act certain ways is because that's what our society has told them men are attracted to. It gets down to the fact that what they all really want is to be loved. Guarding against women only depressed and drained me. I learned not to overthink it, but just respond when I interact with them.

"Follow what you feel. Don't be intellectual about it. It'll just make you depressed. What happened with me was that I was wavering from worshipping the creation to hating the creation. The first one meant lusting for them and placing them above God. The second one meant hating a gift from God. And there's one more thing too, I wanted to talk to you about."

I waited as he took a sip of his coffee. He set the cigar down and leaned back in his chair.

"You know, tonight, when I picked you up at the airport? You're still as quiet as you were before we left for Africa. You talked more when we were in Uganda, but it's like you've stepped back into your shell again. There were times back when we were at Pepperdine, when we were all out on the town and we were all talking and laughing and I would look over at you and your mind was off somewhere else. It's like you have trouble staying in the here and now. Do you mind if I ask what you're always thinking about?"

Ryan handed me the cigar. I took a puff and kept the cigar in my fingers. I loved the feeling of a cigar and coffee because every time I smoked one, I was always in the company of my closest friends. "The past, the present and the future. I think a lot about the mission field. I think a lot about the people I've met."

"I can kind of relate to what you're saying," he said. "When I was a missionary in Zambia, the locals once came and knocked on the door of the minister's house, where I was staying. They asked if he was there and I said, 'No, he'll be back later this evening. Maybe tonight.' And they said, 'That's okay; we'll just wait.' So they walked over and sat under a tree and waited until the evening. They came back the next morning."

"Did the minister ever show?" I asked.

"Yeah, eventually. It was normal for them. I mean, what else would they do? They didn't have jobs or somewhere they had to be. Then there was this other time when I made a sandwich and someone knocked on the door. There were two people, and they asked if we had any food because they didn't have any at all. And I said, 'No, we don't, sorry.' I was staying there and, you know, we didn't have a big pantry for those kinds of things.

"So I shut the door and walked back into the kitchen. I picked up my sandwich and started eating it right as they walked by the open window. They just looked at me like this." Ryan dropped his jaw and stared into nothing. "I felt horrible," he continued. "I've never forgotten it. Do you ever think about how we could have been born in Africa, and that could be us over there?"

I handed the cigar back to Ryan and he took a puff off it and handed it back to me. I inhaled the next draw and kept it in my lungs. I closed my eyes and let out the smoke, feeling the concoction spread through my body, lightening my senses. "I think about it all the time," I said. Then I returned the cigar to him and waved it away. "I know one thing, though," I said. "When Frankl taught that love and purpose gives life meaning, he can't be far off."

All the answers to our questions in this life will never come, and our questions will never end. Love is the only thing that makes sense to me. That is the one thing anyone can exercise, whether they are an illiterate shepherd, or a university professor. We can never know enough and we can never love enough. We can learn learn, learn, for eternity, but life is richer when we love, love, love. For love unites us as a human race; inspires us to continue living. I wonder if love's the only thing worth living for. Is that the meaning of life? To simply love no matter the consequences. After Africa, and Eden, I am seeing the life of love and service in a new light.

–Journal

When Ryan and I went back to his apartment, I lay down on his couch and he went to his bedroom where Joanna was already asleep. We were planning to drive up to Big Sur the next day, travel along Pacific Coast Highway and stop at the Hearst Castle.

The next morning I received the phone call.

Chapter 13

"Son," Dad said. "Your Grandpa's in the hospital. They think he had a heart attack at breakfast this morning. He's not doing well. You need to come home now."

I changed my flight and arrived in Nashville that evening. Dad met me at the airport and we drove straight to the hospital. "In one day, your grandpa's already losing his ability to speak clearly. Just yesterday he was talking and laughing with us. Now, he just wants to lay there with his eyes closed and his mouth open. You have to lean over him and make sure he's looking in your eyes to talk with him. That's the only way you know he's listening. And you need to speak loud and clear."

Extended family members gathered around couches and chairs in the hallways of the hospital as the elevator opened and I stepped out. The sterile smell of hospitals, especially in winter, is stomach curling. Hospitals are never good news.

Relatives stood out of my way, allowing a direct path to Grandpa's room. They spoke no words but forced smiles and unremitting stares at my face. Dad led me to Grandpa's room and I stood over his bed. Grandpa looked terribly thin. His chin pointed upward, his mouth open, and his loud breaths filled the room. Caleb stood beside him.

"Dad?" Dad stood over Grandpa and stroked his forehead and hair.

"Uhhg," was his response.

"Finn's here."

"Uumm," he replied. Grandpa opened his eyes slightly. They were a cloudy-gray.

"Grandpa?" I said. Caleb and Dad walked out of the room and shut the door behind them. I took a seat on a stool beside his bed and buried my face in his chest. Grandpa raked his fingers across the top of my head. "I love you," he mumbled.

I raised my head, surprised he was conscious. "I love you, too."

"Mms your flight?"

I shook my head, almost smiling at such a simple and untimely question. "I'm sorry I stayed gone for so long."

"You did the best you could with the knowledge you had. That's the best anyone can ask for."

"What are we going to do?" I thought aloud.

Grandpa drew a deep breath, and his voice was now a whisper. "You're going to live, Finn. Keep on living. Just live." He moved his hand to the side of my face and patted it. "Don't miss out on life, son, by mourning it away." He took another lungful of air, then exhaled. "The world needs you, Clayton." He patted my shoulder.

"Don't worry about me. We've all been dying since the day we were born. It's just my time to go."

And at some point that night, he told me, "If you pour out your love to others and genuinely love people, you'll find the healing you seek. When you're my age, and you look back on your life, the greatest moments that stand out will be the times you poured yourself out for others. Don't miss that."

We spoke of other things, but those are the words I remember most. He relaxed his hands and body not long after that. I took his hand, sandwiched it in between mine and I lay my head on his arm. The next thing I knew, Dad was nudging me. "Wake up, son," he whispered. It was evening and Grandpa was sound asleep. "Let's go home and let you take a shower and get some rest." I did so. And during the night, Grandpa passed away.

I'm not sure why, but I didn't cry for him after that day, nor did I see anyone else do so. We knew the day would come soon, even though it happened unexpectedly. It didn't seem like a goodbye but more like a see-you-later. Everyone in our family shared a common joy in having the privilege of knowing him. We all dwelt on that rather than our loss.

As the days crawled toward the deadline to sign the papers for Vanderbilt, a thick heaviness fell around me. I never understood, before then, the concept of depression. As a boy, life was full and vibrant with an entire world just waiting to be discovered. It was inconceivable to me how people could come to a place in their lives where they never wanted to leave their house. How they would choose to avoid spending time with loved ones, not enjoy listening to loud music with friends, not want to go dancing or hang out in places where pretty girls were. But I understood it then. I wanted none of those things anymore. If I died the next day, so what?

I had everything I imagined would make me happy. I was raised in a good family with loving parents and a grandpa, I had a graduate degree, and I had friends and a brother in my life who loved me. I had traveled the world, and I was in good health. I was surrounded by green pastures, while the comforts and conveniences of the city were only a short drive away. I had a roof over my head and plenty to eat. But only feelings of drought and loss permeated my being.

Caleb visited home from Texas, where he was a successful businessman. Though my heart was delighted to be near him again, I felt an incredible sense of loneliness. Something seemed out of place, wrong, amiss; like a bad dream wherein you're aware that you're asleep, but you can do nothing to wake up.

I went for walks across the fields in my cozy, cotton-knit shirt, my worn-out jeans, and my cowboy boots. I would stand at our pasture fence and watch the sun set. One day, it was a red ball, trailed by pink ripples; then the next, it was a yellow bulb, shining against gold-dusted clouds. Though it seemed as if heaven was on the other side of the hill, for some reason, the sunset was sad. At night, I would sit in the rocking chair by the fire with a cup of coffee and a book in my hand, a practice I had grown to love over the years. But what was once refreshing was now depressing. And when I stopped to ask myself what was wrong with me, to see the world as so dull, dark, and worn-out looking, I remembered.

On some days, Eden's face would randomly appear in my mind. It felt as if someone was stacking bricks on my shoulders. Every day the load grew heavier. I tried to remember Grandpa's words. "It will get worse, almost unbearable, just before it gets better." Those words, though, were now of little encouragement.

One evening after Christmas, I was standing in my bedroom looking at all my high school pictures and high school basketball trophies that decorated the walls. High School had been a world so small and centered on me, where everyone in town knew my name and jersey number, a world that began and ended at Reedy Creek.

Dad passed by my door and stopped and smiled. "Reminiscing, son?"

"It doesn't even seem like the same life," I answered.

"It doesn't?"

I shook my head. The trophies now seemed to be only metal and plastic, reminding me of a boy I once was, the joyous innocence and naïve bravery in how he believed that one day he would set out to explore the world and conquer it.

I missed that kid.

When I walked out of my bedroom, I was reminded that I would soon leave home again to enter another academic institution and step right back into the world as I left it. A newspaper called and requested an interview about my experiences in Africa. A magazine asked me to write an article on how to build an effective street children rehab program. Universities were inviting me to speak and offering payment. Those were the things I had always wanted: to be a professor, write, give talks, travel and serve like Grandpa. But now, all I really wanted to do was curl up in a ball and cry.

Maybe I could wake and realize Pepperdine, Africa and Grandpa's death were all just a dream. I would say to myself, "Wait a second. Did all that actually happen? Did I really live in California and Africa and did I truly fall in love with a woman?" I would then shake away such thoughts because they were, in fact, just a dream. Then, life would be joyous again! I would find and marry a southern belle who wore cowgirl boots and cotton sundresses and skirts, and she would go barefoot during the summertime. She would call me Baby and Honey, and I would call her Darlin' and Sugarplum. I'd say, "Come over here, Sugarplum, and give me a kiss." And she would.

Chapter 14

I called Vanderbilt the next day.

"May I speak with Dr. Willis?"

"One moment," a diplomatic lady replied.

A fuzzy pop and then, "This is Dr. Willis."

"Dr. Willis? This is Clayton Fincannon."

"Yes, Clayton. Did you receive the documents in the mail?"

"Yes, sir. But I've decided to turn down the offer. I'm going back to Africa."

Dr. Willis asked that I let him know if I changed my mind, because the offer would still stand. But I knew where I stood. Kony had to be stopped. I had fallen in love with the people of East Africa and I couldn't say no anymore.

Money still remained from Grandpa's funding, and I knew I could raise more when I needed it.

I emailed William and told him about my decision, but also about the additional mission the embassy requested. I copied Gunnery Sergeant Duncan. William replied a few days later, "We can't wait to see you again Clayton!" The sergeant also replied, asking me to come by his office once I settled. As soon as I received those messages, I ordered airfare to return immediately. Mom and Dad said little while I packed. They didn't want me to go, but they understood. They thought it was because I was trying to deal with the loss of Grandpa.

Would life have been fulfilling for me if I had taken the position at Vanderbilt? Of course. Teaching is a very respectable vocation. But my classes would be required for most of the students, not chosen, thus many students would find it boring. Vanderbilt could easily find another professor.

Or, I could return to East Africa and continue helping a people I had grown to love and had asked me to stay.

During my last night in town, I went to bed early so I could wake and catch my morning flight. I had finished stuffing some remaining clothes into my backpack when Caleb knocked on the door, and came in to say goodnight. He stayed current with world affairs. He knew of Joseph Kony and the rebels in Uganda, and about Al-Queda in Kenya. Caleb leaned against the wall with his arms crossed. "So what exactly will you be doing when you go back?"

"I'll be working with the street kids again and making trips back to Kampala to help out with some projects there. I'll help with the refugees, things like that." Caleb was my brother, but I felt it best to keep the meeting with the sergeant to myself. "A lot of the missionaries and expats have left because of all the stuff that's going on, so they need our help."

Caleb pushed himself off the wall. "So, let me get this right. People are leaving because of all the crap that's taking place, and you're going in?" Caleb and I both knew the media only portrays the attention-grabbers that take place in other countries. Therefore, no country has problems in every single city or region. "Why do you want to do this kind of thing?"

"Risking my life for social justice makes me feel alive. And I need that."

"But you've been gone for so long. We worry about you over there." His words meant a lot to me, but they weren't enough to change my mind.

"Listen," I said. "I miss the orphans. We're all like family over there. I don't mean they compare to you and Mom and Dad. You know they don't. But when I was over there, every morning when I woke up, I knew where I was and what I was doing. I had a purpose. I was like a brother to them, a teacher, and they needed me. And there's other things."

"Like what?"

"I don't want to talk about it," I answered, pausing for a moment. But because Caleb had pressed the issue, I said, "I just came back from Africa, Caleb. I talked to people whose kids were burned alive in barrels because they were from the wrong tribe. I ate with their parents. I became friends with them. Street kids were starving, had gone days without eating. We bought them food and then they turned around and offered their food to us. Then I come back here and Aunt Sarah wants to know when I'll start dating and looks at me strangely when I say I'm not interested. Uncle Terry asks me when I'll stop being a missionary and get a real job. And someone laughed at me in town the other day when they heard I don't own a car. And all along there are all these disasters in Africa. They're literally begging for help. And I respond by turning my back on them? I can always return home. Always. But I can't always return to Africa. If the rebels aren't stopped . . ."

I ceased speaking at that point. I was afraid Caleb would decipher that there was more to the story than I was sharing.

"You've seen a lot, Finn, and I'm sorry all this has happened. But does any of it have to do with that girl from Pepperdine?" I huffed and lay down on the bed. When Caleb realized he wouldn't get much of a response out of me, he changed the subject. "While you were in Africa these past years, I wore that cross necklace every day you got for me in Romania. I didn't take it off until you were home."

"Really?"

"Yeah, bro. I was worried about you over there. You can bet that I'll be wearing it until you come back home."

"I think I could use your prayers instead of you wearing a necklace."

We both chuckled. "I'm taking you to the airport tomorrow while Mom and Dad are at work. So I'll see you in the morning."

"Goodnight."

"Goodnight," he said.

"Hey, will you turn off the light, please?"

Caleb flipped the switch when he opened the door. Then he turned back and said, "Clay?"

"Yeah?"

"So what did you think about it?"

"About what?"

"You know, being in love. What did you think about it?"

I thought for a moment, searching for the appropriate words. "It was everything I imagined it would be . . . and everything I never expected."

Caleb smiled, his mind, I presume, reliving the memories he and his wife shared. Then he closed the door behind him. I wanted to stay home and I wanted to go to Africa. I wanted to live so I could be with Mom, Dad and Caleb. And I wanted to die, so I could meet God and ask Him why the world is in the shape it's in.

The next morning, Caleb knocked on my door. "Hey bro, before we leave, you need to go over to Grandpa's study and see if there are any books you want. We'll be cleaning out his house and moving all of his stuff into storage tomorrow."

I nodded and rolled out of bed, slipped on my

boots, jeans, and a coat, and walked over to Grandpa's house. I slid the key in and the door creaked a little when I opened it. Scents of thirty years rushed through my nose. I was reminded that Grandpa would never greet me in his house again. No more standing and waiting at his open office door while he finished reading the last paragraphs from a book. No more seeing him juggle his pipe and drop bits of loose tobacco onto his vest. No more letters or talks around the fire. No more, *I love you,* or glasses of sweet tea in Mason jars.

I shook the thoughts away and entered his study. Bits of shattered glass gleamed on the floor at the opposite corner of his desk. I walked over to see what picture frame had fallen, and when I turned the corner, lying there was our Mason jar. No letter. Just brokenness.

I pulled out a broom and dustpan from the hall closet, and swept up the tiny fragments and dumped them into the garbage can. The handle and rim, and a large portion of the jar's body, was still intact. I took it home and placed it in one of my dresser drawers.

I decided to keep the broken pieces. Not throw them away. They were a part of who I was now.

When I shut the drawer, I caught a glimpse of myself in the mirror that stood on top of my dresser. That mirror had watched me grow up. The image looking back at me was no longer a boy. I didn't feel old enough to be a man, but I was no longer a child, either. To be caught somewhere in-between feels awkward, like being sixteen and your feet still not reaching the pedal.

Caleb's voice echoed down the hall from his bedroom. "Are you ready, Clay?"

"Yeah." I took my loaded backpack into the garage and dropped it into Caleb's car seat. I hugged Mom and Dad goodbye. When Caleb and I arrived at the airport, we hugged each other, and I threw the pack over my shoulder. "Okay," I said.

"Love you, Clay."

"Love you too, bro." When I entered the doors of the airport, I turned around to find Caleb's gaze following me; a look of worry and pride. And instead of feeling sad over our parting, I chose to be thankful for our lives together: for Caleb's loyalty, my parents' love, and for Grandpa's life and guidance he shared with me through the Mason jar.

PART IV

Eden closed *The Mason Jar*. Six hours had passed, yet she had finished it in one sitting. She stood and set Finn's book down on the end table and walked into the kitchen. She ran water into her coffee mug to keep the tea from staining it, then gripped the counter and leaned forward on her hands, remembering times with Finn she had forgotten. Her mind and emotions exhausted, she tilted her head and massaged her neck with her hands.

Homecoming, she thought. Finn might be there. Dad will know what to do. Eden pulled out her cell phone and looked at the world clock in her drop menu. It was six o'clock in the morning in Colorado, and she knew her dad would be awake.

"Hey, sweetie," Mr. Hadley said.

"Hey, dad."

"How's your day?"

"It's good," she answered, trying to press through the formalities.

"Work was good?" he asked.

"Yeah," she said, hesitating, unsure of how she would relate the contents in the book she had just read. "Some paintings were late yesterday but that was alright. Listen," she said abruptly. "I need to ask your advice about something."

"Sure."

"It's about Clayton Fincannon. Do you remember him?"

"Clayton Fincannon, Clayton . . . oh, was that the boy who had dinner with us that time?"

"Yeah. He wrote a book about me."

"What do you mean he wrote a book about you?"

"He wrote a book about me, about our time together."

"Well, what did he say?"

"He said good things. Stuff I didn't realize he felt."

"He mentions your name?"

"No, he changed it. I don't know, I just wasn't expecting something like this." Eden reached behind her head and pulled her hair away from her face and off her shoulder, letting it fall comfortably down her back. Finn's words had left her nostalgic for their time together and revived fond memories of Pepperdine. But reading about herself from another's perspective . . . she wasn't sure how to respond.

"Okay, well what's it about?"

"Just about our time together and stuff he did later."

"Like what?"

"He went to Africa and spent some time with his grandfather."

"And the book's good?"

"Yeah, it's good."

"Can I read it?" he asked.

"I guess, I don't know." Eden laughed a little. "I can send it to you, I guess."

"So what's on your mind?"

"Well, he might be at Pepperdine this weekend for Homecoming."

"You're still going, right, and stopping here?"

"I've decided to, yes."

"Great! Well, how do you feel? Do you still have feelings for him?"

"Of course I do. But I thought he hated me."

"Does he know that?"

"I don't know. He talks about some letters he wrote me. But I never received anything."

How would Finn respond when he saw her? Would he know she'd read his book? Maybe Ryan told him Joanna had sent it to her.

"Well, why don't you go to Pepperdine, and if he's there, talk to him?"

"What if he doesn't want to talk to me? What if he does hate me?"

"I doubt that, honey. If he cared for you, he'll probably be glad to see you. If he still loved you all those years, I doubt you have anything to be worried about. He might not feel the same way now, but he'll still care about you." Eden thought for a moment. "Are you still there?"

"Yeah. So Pepperdine," Eden said, bringing the discussion back to the reason she called. "I'll see you tomorrow, then."

"So will I receive a copy of the book?" he asked. It sounded like he was grinning.

"Mmm. I don't know," she replied, her words trailing off into a laugh.

He laughed, too. "Okay, well let me know how it goes."

"I will. Thanks, Dad. Love you."

"Love you, too."

Eden had visited Pepperdine two or three times to watch friends graduate but she never attended any of the homecomings. Neither had Finn.

The next day, stepping out of a taxi in Colorado Springs on a beautiful spring day, Eden paid the driver and approached her parents' home carrying a small suitcase, purse, and a sheathed painting.

Ms. Alice, a maid and nurse helping care for her dad, opened the front door. "I believe you're still growing, child," Alice remarked.

Eden laughed and they hugged. "It's good to see you, Alice."

"Your dad's on the phone."

Eden could hear her dad in the kitchen, talking to the pharmacist. She laid her belongings on the floor by the door and climbed the stairs to her bedroom. Eden rummaged through her chest of drawers, looking for Finn's letters. Nothing. She heard a rap on her door and turned to see her dad smiling at her.

"Hey sweetie, you looking for your mail?"

She skipped over and hugged him.

"Check your mother's room. I haven't gone through her things."

"Dad," Eden answered, concerned.

Mr. Hadley held his hands up in defense. "I'm just not ready yet."

The phone rang downstairs.

"Where are you sleeping?" she asked her dad.

"In the guest room."

"Mr. Hadley?" Alice called.

"Yes?" he replied.

"Dr. Blake's on the phone."

"Be right there!" Mr. Hadley kissed his daughter on the forehead. "Be right back."

Eden rushed out of her room and tore apart her mother's chest of drawers, but she still didn't find mail. When she tried to quietly rummage through the kitchen drawers, Mr. Hadley walked into the living room to finish his phone call. Eden searched the family junk drawer near the phone, but found nothing. She gritted her teeth and slammed her fists on the counter, feeling the color rise in her cheeks.

"Hey," her dad said, tapping her shoulder. Off the phone now, he held a plastic sack of old mail, all advertisements and mostly junk mail addressed to Eden. "That's all I could find. They were in your mother's desk drawer." When Eden sifted through the stack, she found a handful of letters from Finn, postmarked Africa.

After hugging her dad at the door, Eden carried her suitcase, purse, and the sheathed painting to the taxi, beginning her trip to the airport.

From the Los Angeles International Airport, Eden texted Joanna that she had arrived. Eden rented a car and drove to the main parking lot at Pepperdine. Some of her classmates would be there, but she hadn't bonded with them like she had Joanna. Most of Eden's sorority sisters were either married and couldn't make it to the reunion, or work was keeping them home.

Joanna, holding her phone, met Eden in the middle of the lot, hugging and laughing. "It's so good to see you," Joanna said as she and Eden squeezed each other. "We'll catch up soon, but let's get inside and get some seats before they're taken."

Over the years, they had spoken on the phone about once every six months, but phone conversations and e-mail are nothing compared to engaging in person. Joanna had never prodded Eden about her past or why she left Pepperdine. And Eden was thankful for that.

"Guess what?" Joanna said, tugging at Eden's arm."

"What?"

"With students gone for the semester, we get to stay in our old apartments."

"That's great! Is Finn here?"

"Yep. He's wrapping up a talk."

A main meeting hall called The Fireside Room, in a building adjacent to the cafeteria, was continually hosting events. Joanna and Eden entered a reunion banquet. Caterers and waiters wearing black slacks and polos passed back and forth between tables, refilling people's drinks and taking away finished plates of gourmet meats and vegetables. Helium balloons rose from tables adorned with orange and blue tablecloths, Pepperdine's school colors. Candles and small glass bowls of chocolates decorated the tables. Signs announcing Homecoming covered the walls. Most of the chairs were filled, except two next to Ryan.

The lights were dimmed and hundreds of alumni were listening to Finn speak at a podium on-stage. He wore a black suit and white dress shirt. His black necktie was loosened at the knot for comfort. He was still well-built and in shape, and had grown a neatly trimmed beard. Ten years had passed since she last saw him. His hair had thinned some, but other than that, he looked the same.

As Finn delivered his speech, a cartoon played on a projector screen depicting the story. "For example, some years ago, a Western company entered Honduras and gave away free shoes. In doing so, they destroyed the local shoemaker's business. Later, rebels entered that village, stole the shoes, killed people who stood in their way, and then sold the shoes on the black market. The way we help without hurting is through micro-finance, or microlending.

"We enter the Honduras village, meet with the elders, and the elders select an experienced farmer. That farmer takes business classes and is awarded a loan to purchase property, farm equipment, coffee seeds, and he hires people from his own village. As the coffee grows, he pays back the loan through affordable payments. No one else in the village can receive a loan until that first loan's repaid in full.

"So the villagers rally together to help out until the loan's repaid. Microlending has a ninety-eight percent success rate. When he pays back the loan, he's eligible for a larger loan. The two percent failures are due to natural disasters, or because a child in the village became sick and the money was used toward medical expenses. In these cases, the debt is forgiven. This concept, microlending, won the 2006 Nobel Peace Prize."

When Finn finished his talk, he received a standing ovation, and people waited in line to speak with him. Party music began playing on the loud speakers, pie and coffee was distributed, and voices of alumni, catching up with old friends and new ones, filled the room. Finn would simply nod and offer an appreciative smile and handshake to people. He didn't glory in the limelight. He was just doing his duty. But he didn't smile a lot. He was different. Sad.

Finn spoke with Dr. Daniels. Faculty and alumni passed by and shook hands with him, smiling and patting his back. Oz and Oz's wife, Shana, a blonde of average build, intelligent and joyful, talked among a group of alumni. Katie stood in a different group, watching Finn from afar; her crush appeared to be as strong as ever.

Finn found Oz and patted his shoulder. "Listen, Dr. Daniels wants to introduce me to some more people. If I'm not back in ten minutes, would you come get me?"

"Sure."

"I didn't come here to give talks and do meet-and-greets. I came to hang out with my friends. When you see Ryan, can you tell me? I want to make sure we all have breakfast tomorrow."

"Ten minutes," Oz answered, checking his phone.

"Thanks," Finn said and rejoined Dr. Daniels.

Eden and Joanna made their way to a handful of open seats around a table. Ryan stood and kissed Joanna and hugged Eden. When Oz saw her he couldn't believe his eyes.

"I'll be right back," Oz whispered to Shana. Oz walked to Ryan's table. Eden, having just sat down, sprang from her chair and hugged Oz.

"Oz, how are you?"

Oz hesitated a moment, but returned the hug and withdrew quickly. "What are you doing here, Eden?"

"I came to see Finn. How is he?"

"I don't think that's a good idea," Oz said. "You hurt him badly."

"Is he well?" she asked, worried.

"Define well," was Oz's response.

"Oz," Finn called, approaching him. Oz, blocking Finn's view, whipped around. "Any word from—" Oz dropped his eyes. "What is it?" Finn asked. Oz lifted his eyes to the girl behind him and stepped away.

When Finn saw her, he froze. Ryan and Joanna sat, watching the entire ordeal, but Oz left, rejoining Shana.

Finn believed that one day he'd see her again. But not like this. Just showing up. She was as lovely as Finn remembered. She was more mature now, with much life experience showing in her eyes. She was wiser, he could tell, and maybe even had experienced some pain. The way she stood, with her arms gently crossed, took him back to their first night together when they said goodbye at her car, outside his apartment at Drescher.

Then he remembered receiving the news of her marriage. And he could no longer ignore that in their ten years apart, not once had she called or written to explain what happened. Finn assumed she wanted nothing to do with him. The fact that she was even standing there, willing to engage him, was almost unbearable. His heart plummeted from intial shock into utter hatred and bitterness.

"Hello, Finn," Eden said, watching his eyes and lips, searching for anything that might provide an inclination as to what he was thinking.

"Hello, Eden," he returned. "I see you're not wearing a ring anymore," he smirked. "What did you do? Leave him a note?"

"Finn," Dr. Daniels interrupted, patting Finn's back. "You remember President Benton?" Finn acknowledged the president and shook his hand. "Do you mind if we join you?"

"No, of course not," Ryan said. People shifted their chairs, making room. Ryan added two chairs for Dr. Daniels and the president. Then he pulled out two more for Finn and Eden. Ryan took the seat beside Finn, letting Eden sit beside Joanna. Now, Eden and Finn sat opposite each other.

"So what's everyone doing these days?" President Benton asked.

"Joanna and I are in real estate," Ryan answered.

"I just moved to London," Eden added.

"Just?" Finn asked. "Where've you been?"

Eden wondered if he was preparing another poisonous dart.

"Working as a nurse in Colorado."

"I wanted to tell you, Finn," President Benton said. "Great talk."

"Thank you."

"I wish Chaplain Metcalf could have heard your speech," Dr. Daniels added. "He thought a lot of you."

Joanna shot her eyes at Eden, but Eden's and Finn's eyes were glued on each other's. Eden searched his expression for any trace of love or compassion. But all he could return was a glare.

"How's he doing, anyway?" Finn asked Dr. Daniels, breaking eye contact with Eden for the first time.

"He passed a few years back, from cancer," Dr. Daniels replied.

"I'm sorry to hear that," answered Finn. "I wish there were more people like him." Finn's and Eden's eyes met again.

"We're having a faculty reception tomorrow afternoon," President Benton told Finn. "I told some people you might stop by."

"Sure," Finn nodded.

President Benton's wife tapped her husband on the shoulder.

"Darling, there's some people I'd like you to meet." The president and Dr. Daniels stood and shook everyone's hand.

"We'll see you tomorrow," President Benton said to Finn.

"Okay."

Katie, having joined the group after the interruption, touched Finn lightly on his arm.

"Finn, this gentleman wants to meet you." A young man, an alumni, shook Finn's hand.

"Hi, Clayton. My wife loved *The Mason Jar*,"

he said and pointed to a woman engaging friends. "She'd be so pleased if you took some time to meet her."

He hated Eden now, but he couldn't ignore how drawn he was to her. He didn't want to leave her. He wanted answers.

"That'll be fine," Finn answered solemnly. But it was the last thing he wanted to do.

Katie nudged the small of Finn's back and escorted him toward the young woman. Oz joined Finn's other side, handing him a drink and waiting for him to speak. But when Finn said nothing, Oz kept his silence and stood by him.

"Eden!" squealed a former classmate, whose face and name Eden couldn't remember. "I haven't seen you in years!" the girl said, hugging her. "How are you?"

"I'm well. And you?"

Eden glanced back at Finn but he had disappeared into the crowd.

Saturday at lunchtime, Joanna, Eden, and Shana waited at a picnic table outside the Malibu Country Mart. There, pastel-painted ice cream parlors, coffee shops, boutiques, and upscale restaurants encircled a playground where Malibu moms brought their children to play.

From branches, seagulls watched the park for meals left unattended. Sparrows awaited dropped crumbs. And lapdogs restrained by designer leashes barked at the squirrels chasing each other in the trees.

Joanna, Shana, and Eden waited on their lunch orders. Oz and Ryan brought drinks from across the street. The restaurant was a family-owned café that served farm-raised food and organic drinks of every variety one could imagine. Oz and Ryan had just arrived from spending the morning with Finn.

"Forty-five!" a barista yelled from the café. Eden, with her ticket in hand, left the group to get her sandwich.

Ryan and Oz handed out the drinks.

"Where's Finn?" Joanna demanded.

"He's at President Benton's," Ryan replied, with a quizzical brow. "He said he'd see us at the party tonight."

"He didn't say anything at breakfast?"

"He told us to stay out of it," Oz said.

"He's being a jerk," Joanna snapped.

"No, he's not," Oz answered. "He's protecting himself."

"Protecting himself?" Joanna replied. "Did you hear how he spoke to her last night?"

"Finn's hurting," Oz reminded her. "We act like that when we're hurting. It's a defense mechanism."

"But it was ten years ago."

"Have you forgotten what she did?" Oz said. "And then she just shows up like that? She didn't even write him all those years ago."

"She didn't know about the letters."

"What do you mean?"

"Her mother had a stroke and never sent them."

"Even if that's the case," Oz replied, "it doesn't excuse what she did."

"But you don't know the whole story," Joanna answered.

"Well, what is the story?"

Joanna pressed her hands to her temples and huffed.

Faculty and staff buzzed about the president's home, some inside talking and lingering near refreshment tables. Others stood at the edge of the back yard enjoying the magnificent view of the ocean. The sun warmed the crème-colored, Mediterranean-styled home with its red-clay roof and roman archways. Waiters dressed in white, crisp shirts replenished punch bowls and food trays.

Finn and Dr. Daniels shook hands with various people as they made their way out the back door. A faculty couple greeted Finn as he stopped by one of the tables for a fresh glass of punch.

"We're looking forward to your talk tonight, Clayton."

"Thank you," Finn said. "It will be my last." Then, he and Dr. Daniels strolled to the yard's edge to watch the sun begin its slow descent behind the cliffs and palm trees.

"Your last talk, huh?" said Dr. Daniels.

"Yep. I'm done."

Dr. Daniels pulled out a cigar from his inner coat pocket and snipped off its end with a cigar cutter. Finn took a flask from his pocket and spiked his punch.

"How's your grandfather?"

"He passed."

"Oh, Finn. I'm sorry to hear that."

"It's okay. He lived a full life."

Dr. Daniels lit his cigar and puffed it until the end was fully lit. Finn turned and watched the golden sun evolve to red.

"Oz said you're not teaching anymore. That you returned from Africa and moved into your grandfather's house. That you've become a recluse."

"Oz exaggerates. I'm writing full time"

"Will you ever attend Vanderbilt again?"

"I doubt it."

"I thought that's what you always wanted."

"It was, ten years ago."

"Dreams change, don't they?"

"Yes, sir."

Dr. Daniels took a draw from his cigar and blew it to the side. "When you walk on this campus, everyone knows who you are. If they don't, they've heard of you."

"I don't care about that," Finn answered.

"I know. And that's why you shouldn't stop. You teach people not to do humanitarian work if they can't do it right. No one's heard that before. And your reasons are excellent."

"There's plenty of material teaching it."

"But they haven't read the books," Dr. Daniels replied. "And they don't have the experience. You do. And you can teach."

"I'm done." Finn, having drunk the last bit of punch, poured the flask's remaining whiskey into his glass and downed it, too.

"You know what the people at World Vision told me?" Dr. Daniels continued. "When *The Mason Jar* was released, contributions to their microlending programs tripled. All because of your book."

"A book you still haven't read," Finn answered, cocking his chin.

"Yeah, sorry about that," he replied. "It's on my list."

"It's alright," Finn said. "Most men don't like love stories."

"I know someone you could write your next love story about. Chaplain Metcalf. Now, he was a romantic. Years ago, he came here and pledged his love to a girl. I never met her. But they say she dropped out of school, just like that," he said, snapping his fingers, "and went home with him. Yeah, he—"

"What did you just say?" Finn interrupted him.

"I said he pledged his love to a girl here and she left with him."

"What was her name?" Finn returned.

Dr. Daniels furrowed his brow, looking away. "I don't remember."

"Was it Eden?"

"Yeah!"

A waiter crashed a plate of dishes into a table. Dr. Daniels spun around, and when he turned back, Finn had dropped his glass and had already crossed the yard.

"Finn!" Dr. Daniels called after him. "Where you going?"

Light thunder and music filled the air as Finn stepped off the shuttle, which dropped him and others off at a private party at a home in Malibu. Two hundred alumni and friends gathered across the lawn at an outdoor bar, eating and drinking. Others hung out near the infinity swimming pool and watched the view of the city lights. A catering company provided hosts, hostesses, and bartenders with top liquors and the choicest wines from Napa Valley.

Finn spotted Ryan and Oz talking among a group of young men a few steps away from the pool. Their women stood near the diving board and bar. Finn scanned the crowd for Eden. And then he saw her. Dressed in a sharp gray pants suit, her hair was pinned into a French twist, and she looked as lovely as ever. Finn both loved and hated it. He stepped toward her, but Katie, who was standing near Eden and anticipated

Finn's move, intercepted Eden and pretended to be excited to see her.

"Eden!" Katie exclaimed, grasping Eden's shoulders. "How's Colorado?"

"It's good, Katie," Eden replied, kindly. "Thanks for asking. Where are you now?"

Oz, witnessing Katie's little fiasco, scoffed and turned back to his friends. Finn, blocked by Katie's move, joined Oz and Ryan.

"I can't stay long," Finn said, shaking their hands. "I have one last talk at seven."

"That's in fifteen minutes," Ryan interjected.

"Yeah, I know," Finn replied, apologetically. "But it's my last one. Ever."

"Whoa," Oz said, cocking his head back and waving at the air between them. "Do you usually drink this much before a talk?"

Finn smirked and returned his eyes to Eden. During her conversation with Katie, she had glanced toward the men, her eyes met Finn's, and they locked. Why did she have to have such beautiful brown eyes? he thought. Both tried to away, but an unseen force captured them. The thunder grew louder.

"So," Oz said, touching Finn's shoulder to get his attention. "We were talking with these guys and they're about to build an orphanage in Guatemala. I told them to talk to you."

"We have the funding," one of the young men said. "But we really don't know where to begin."

Finn watched Eden again.

"Finn," Oz said, pulling him back into the conversation.

"Read the book *When Helping Hurts* by Corbett and Fikkert," Finn replied, checking back in. "It'll teach you all the principles you need to know. I'd read that before doing anything. Anyone in humanitarian work or missions needs to read it."

"Thanks," the young man said, glancing at his friend. "We'll do that."

A light rain fell. Everyone took shelter in the house and under awnings. Others boarded shuttles to return to their vehicles. Finn's phone rang. An unknown number.

"Hello?" Finn answered, plugging his opposite ear with his finger.

"Mr. Fincannon?"

"Yeah."

"I work in Kenya with the Colburns."

"Yes," Finn replied.

"Their relatives gave me your number. William Colburn passed away while visiting family in Nashville." Finn rubbed his face with his hand and paused for a moment of silence.

"Mr. Fincannon?" the man asked, making sure Finn was still on the phone.

"When's the funeral?"

"In two days. In Nashville."

"Okay. I'll fly in tomorrow."

"That's great!" the man replied. "I'll tell—"

Finn ended the call and checked the time. Six-fifty p.m. His last speech was in ten minutes. He searched the crowd again for Eden. He didn't see her with Katie, watching him from under an awning.

"I have to change my flight and I still have that speech," Finn said to Ryan and Oz. "I'll get with you guys later."

Frustrated and torn between his responsibilities and finding Eden, Finn passed by the pool on his way to the shuttle. Eden burst out from under the awning, into the rain, chasing after Finn. When Katie followed, Oz snatched her arm and whirled her around to face him.

"Leave them alone, Katie!"

"Let me go!" she screamed, jerking her arm free and pushing past him. "White trash!"

The blood surged through Oz's veins, taking him back to his days in Tuscaloosa. He tore after her, clutched her shoulders, and hurled her into the pool.

Alumni filled the shuttle. The rain was pouring heavily now. Finn bounded down the steps leading to the curb.

"Finn!" Eden called from behind him.

Finn was now only steps from the shuttle doors.

"Finn, STOP!" she screamed.

Finn froze and closed his eyes. Other alumni passed by Finn with coats over their heads, and boarded the shuttle. Now the shuttle was full, and the driver, seeing that the young man had stopped, shut the doors and left.

Finn turned and faced her. She was within arm's reach, and both were drenched by the rain.

"Did you marry Chaplain Metcalf?" Finn shouted above the pounding of the rain against the pavement.

"I did," she stated, unashamed.

"He's obviously great with words."

"You don't know the whole story."

With the rain now streaming down their faces, Finn directed them to shelter under a magnolia tree at the corner of the driveway. The thunder rose louder.

"Well, I've waited ten years," he said, sardonically. "So let's hear it, if you can tell the truth."

"With the way you looked at me last night and the way you're talking to me now, with so much judgment and hatred—"

"Judgment and hatred?!" Finn stormed. "All those years, never once did you contact me. Was I just some college fling for you?!"

"No! Mother's condition got worse and she had a stroke. She never gave me your letters. I wanted to reach out but I—"

"You could have told Joanna or Ryan. You—"

"It's not that easy!"

"You're lying!"

"No! The person you were in college would

understand. But not this person you've become now."

"Is that right?"

"That's right!"

"Well, the woman I knew in college would never run off with a guy she barely knew only to leave me a courtesy note!"

"You don't want to hear the truth. You've yelled nothing but accusations," Eden added. "You want to hate me!"

Finn seized Eden's arms, jerking her to him. "Fine!" he growled, gritting his teeth. "Tell me."

Eden's eyes filled with tears. "You're hurting me." Even after the warning, the hurt and anguish had filled his heart to such a degree he could barely loosen his grip. "Let me go, Finn!" she shouted, her eyes flashing. His hands loosened and she yanked free. "You're wrong," she said, the emotion catching in her throat and chest.

"You're wrong," she said. "You see, I knew and loved Victor Metcalf my entire life. And I was engaged to him, even before I met you at Pepperdine."

Those words, along with the crackling of thunder, stunned Finn, leaving him speechless. And Eden ran through the rain and back to the house.

Hours had passed and Finn lay on his bed in a fresh set of clothes; jeans and a white linen shirt hand-stitched by a Kumulu woman from Congo.

He had changed his flight to seven o'clock the next morning. His bags were packed. His last talk finished. But now he couldn't sleep. He got up and paced the empty apartment. He lifted his half empty bottle of whiskey, examined it, and dropped it in the trash. Alcohol had added nothing of value to his life.

He peered out his bedroom window, out over the coast. A romantic glow from the moon lit his face and room. That room. That apartment. There, Finn remembered their Valentine's night, so long ago.

The journey to ten o'clock that night, ten years ago, had dragged along. His class on the poetry of Longfellow and Emerson involved an intense discussion as usual, and Finn thought his brain would explode. After class, he had jetted to his apartment, hopped in the shower, dried his hair, and put on his best dress shirt and slacks. His bed was unmade and books and papers were strewn everywhere. He cleaned it up. Ryan had left dishes to drain on the towel after his own dinner date with Joanna hours before. Crumbs were scattered across the counters. The garbage hadn't been emptied. Finn felt his frustration rising, but was sure Ryan forgot.

Eden called and sounded impatient on the phone, so Finn told her to come over while he continued cleaning. Ryan called and said he needed to drop by and grab a book from his room. Then the doorbell rang.

"Who's out there? No one's home!" Finn teased. He opened the door to Eden laughing. She wore a calico top and her hair was waved, perhaps from a curling iron. Her lips were painted carnation red. Finn turned away to finish the phone conversation with Ryan, and Finn felt Eden's gaze and smile.

When Finn ended the call, he turned off his phone and hugged her. "You look beautiful." She smiled, and gently kissed Finn's lips. Then she sat at the living room table beside the bay windows, which overlooked the navy abyss of the ocean, shimmering under the moon. A necklace of lights flickered along the coast.

Eden handed Finn wine glasses and a Miles Davis CD. On the table, Finn placed a bowl of chopped dark chocolate in a nest of white flowers, with purple star-burst blossoms in their centers. She lifted one of the flowers and smiled. "Where did these come from?"

"Don't tell the Pepperdine gardeners."

Eden laughed, and Finn opened the wine at the kitchen counter. Given that his cork screw was broken, he thought of stepping out of the kitchen and removing his shirt, in case he got wine on it. But he didn't want to leave the room because any second away from her would have been a terrible loss. With steady pulling, out came the cork with a splash of wine on his shirt. He shook his head, gritted his teeth, smiled away the self-scorn, and turned around to see Eden biting back a laugh. "I'll be right back."

Finn removed his shirt in his bedroom, threw it into the corner, and grabbed another from his closet. Tucked in? No, tucked out, he thought to himself. No, tucked in. It looks better.

"Nice," Eden murmured sensually when Finn returned to the kitchen. The way she drew out the syllable sped his pulse up. He felt the blush creep up his neck and cheeks. She looked at him as though she was a lover who had been separated from him for longer than she could bear. He loved the fact that when he turned away, he could feel her eyes scanning his body.

Finn inserted Miles Davis' CD *Kind of Blue* into his laptop and set it on the kitchen counter. Then he turned off the kitchen light. He sat beside her and poured two glasses of red wine, and they took each other's hands. The vivacity radiating from her face when she looked at him, the reciprocal admiration she felt that was evident as she leaned in naturally to take his hands, was intoxicating.

The first sip of wine was too tangy for their freshly brushed teeth, evident by their sour facial expressions. They both laughed and wiped their mouths. But the rest of the wine went down smoothly. Their hands explored each other's face. Her fingers slipped down below his ears, caressing his neck. Finn took her hands and cupped them over his cheeks and kissed her wrists. She smiled and looked over his shoulder. "It's as if you really treasure me."

"I do," he said, realizing she obviously didn't understand how much he adored her. She was the most incredible, beautiful creature he had ever encountered. He wanted her in ways he could not begin to describe, and his thoughts would have shamed him if they were known to others. In the past, he had shaken those thoughts away, but he didn't want to anymore. He loved the way she looked at him, and he didn't want that to stop. He had never reacted that way to a woman. He strove to ignore the waves of tingling on his back, and focus on savoring their moment.

When his glass was half empty, he refilled it and leaned over to refill hers, which was already empty. Finn burst out laughing while her body shook in silent laughter.

"I think I've had enough!" she said.

"Do you want to dance?" he asked. They stood and held each other, shifting their weight from foot to foot.

"Do you ever think about where we'll be years from now?" she asked.

"I don't care where I am as long as I'm with the people I love."

Eden nestled her face into his neck. He kissed her forehead. "What are you thinking about?" she whispered.

"Wondering what will happen after graduation. London."

"I'm not accepted yet."

"You'll get in. You'll be at Sotheby's, and no matter what happens, I'll meet you there."

Eden brushed her lips against his neck. Softly. Tenderly. "And after London?" she whispered.

"What do you want?" he asked.

She shrugged her shoulders.

"We can decide where to go next while we're in London. What if we found a cabin somewhere in the Colorado mountains? Engulfed by the woods. No television. The experiences of our everyday lives, our humanitarian work and our teachings could be great education for our children when they're not in school."

"Well, I don't want my children to be too sheltered," she laughed. "And I would need to live near a city." Then she caressed the hair on the back of his head and gazed into his eyes. "Could you do that, Finn? Could you live near a city?"

"Of course. I can live anywhere. Especially if I'm with you." He felt her draw a shaky breath. "Isn't this funny?" he whispered.

"What?" she answered, smiling.

"Here we are planning our lives together, and we've only known each other three months. Are we crazy?"

She sighed through a small laugh and leaned

her forehead on his shoulder. "Things are moving so fast," she whispered. "I feel overwhelmed."

"There's a place in the Bible," Finn said. "Matthew 13:44. There, it reads that when you find a priceless treasure, you'll sell and trade every material possession you have and all earthly comforts in order to attain it. Because you know its worth is incomparable to anything else."

Eden's fingers massaged the back of his neck. "Do you always talk like this?"

"Like what?" he whispered.

"Like you're reading poetry. I like it."

"You know how on our first date, after the Italian restaurant? How we were in my bedroom? I looked out the window and saw our reflection in the mirror. Both of us were wearing white shirts, standing and holding each other. It was perfect, Eden. Just perfect."

With her arms still wrapped around his neck, she drew her head back, then slid her hands down and grabbed the front seam of his shirt and pulled him toward her, pressing her lips into his. Finn submitted, surprised and thankful. When she released him, he pulled her into his embrace and kissed her again. Her knees gave way and her body melted into his arms. It was the closest to perfection that he had ever felt.

The next day, they had journeyed together to Colorado. And then, she vanished.

The door to his apartment opened and closed, pulling him from his daydream. Oz or Ryan, he thought. But in the reflection of the window, a vision of Eden approached him from behind. She held a sheathed painting. Was this a dream? Finn didn't move. But he watched the vision. In the moonlight, she was like an angel.

"I came to give you this," she said, leaving it on his dresser. A letter lay attached. She ran her fingers across it. "I painted it years ago." She started toward his door, but paused a moment and turned back around. "I didn't want a reoccurrence from earlier. And I hoped I could write something that might redeem me from the first letter, which I should never have left all those years ago."

Finn spun around. The package still lay on his dresser but she was gone. Finn ran to his living room window and watched a rental car drive away. Finn ran to his room, removed the letter attached to the sheath, and opened it.

Dear Finn,

As long as I can remember, I was in love with a boy named Victor Metcalf. He grew up next door and our parents were close friends. Our families served in medical missions together every summer. He and I were engaged my senior year of high school, a dream come true for me. And for our families.

Victor graduated from seminary and served in Iraq while I studied in Colorado. He returned home with PTSD. After months of his verbal abuse, and his jealousy over my friends, I couldn't take it any longer, so I called off the engagement and came to Pepperdine. Then I met and fell in love with you.

Victor came to speak at Pepperdine but I stayed away from him. I believed it was over between us, until I visited Colorado. There, I learned he received counseling and the treatment he needed, and he still wanted to marry me. Initially, I told him no. But then he came to Pepperdine and begged for my forgiveness. He said he needed me and that he couldn't live without me.

He had opened a clinic for veterans and wanted me to help him. He promised things could be as they once were. I knew that if I saw or spoke to you again, I'd fall apart. And, I knew that if you discovered why I left, you would have dropped out of Pepperdine to come get me. I was still in love with you, but I was also still in love with him. And I had to make a decision. I was hurt, confused, and I was twenty-two years old.

I wanted to tell you everything, but Victor frantically packed all my belongings, throwing them into his jeep, yelling for me to hurry. He even yanked me away while I fought for the words to write you. Ashamed as I am of all that happened, I was young and didn't feel like I had any other choice.

Leaving you that day was the worst day of my life. If you only knew what I went through. How much I loved you. And how much I still love you.

In regards to why I never reached out to you, I cared for Victor through his sickness. And his death took a large toll on me. I had also seen you in a newsreel in Africa. You were with a girl. Believing you had moved on and probably hated me, I left the past alone.

Finn remembered meeting Chaplain Metcalf at Pepperdine on stage all those years ago. And how he had watched Finn at his table. The chaplain wasn't watching me, Finn thought. He was watching Eden. And months later, when Finn met the chaplain again in the cafeteria, Chaplain Metcalf had said, "I came to see an old friend."

Feeling faint, Finn caught himself on his dresser, but knocked off the sheathed painting, sending it crashing on the floor. He left the letter on his dresser, bent down, lifted the sheath, and pulled out the painting.

There, staring back at him was a magnificent portrait of Finn with Grandpa in his office, with their arms around each other's shoulders. It was painted from Eden's memory of the photograph she had seen on Finn's dresser years ago. Finn rubbed his thumb across Grandpa's face. A strange sensation, like the breaking of the soul, rose from Finn's stomach into his chest and throat. And he burst into tears.

Eden, with damp hair, lay on her bed in her robe. She was holding a Homecoming program and staring up at the ceiling. Joanna tapped on Eden's door. "Are you asleep?"

"No," Eden replied, sitting up. Joanna walked in and sat on the edge of Eden's bed.

"I never meant to hurt him, Joanna," Eden told her. "What he must have went through all those years. I'll never forgive myself for that."

"We were children, Eden," Joanna answered, rubbing her back. "What did we know about anything? I can always get his number from Ryan."

"No," Eden answered, shaking her head. "If he doesn't want to talk to me here, he's not going to want to talk over the phone."

"Let's get some sleep. It'll be fun tomorrow seeing everyone one more time and going to the chapel like we used to. It'll be beautiful; the sunny day, the ocean. We can go for one more tea in Malibu before we have to leave. We'll have a good time." Joanna patted Eden's back. "Okay?"

Three rapid knocks sounded from their front door. Eden and Joanna exchanged a puzzled look. Joanna rushed to the door with Eden following. She peeked into the peephole and opened the door. Katie, wearing dry clothes with her hair still damp, pushed through, with a calm, collected sternness about her.

"I came to see Eden," she barked. Joanna stepped away. "You and Joanna were always so close," Katie said to Eden, gruffly. "But I'm glad I was never from Colorado Springs or Manhattan. There's a snootiness there you can't find anywhere else. But for some reason boys fall for it. What? You're not shocked by my remarks?"

Eden, who was leaning against the wall in the hallway with her arms crossed, pushed herself off the wall. "Not since I read Finn's book. Were you ever our friend?"

"I was until you stole Finn," Katie stated.

"Stole him?" Eden answered. "I didn't even know you liked him!"

"So you would've stopped if you had known?"

"No. Especially now."

"Finn and I've been talking since January. And so when I saw you were after him again, I wanted to come and ask you to stay away from him. Are you surprised that he and I are talking?"

Not missing a beat, Eden replied, "If that's true then why hasn't he said something to—"

"My and Finn's business is our own," Katie shot back.

"If I'm not a threat, then why are you here?"

"Because you confuse him. You get in his head! Now would you please stay away from him?"

"If Finn wanted to be with me, he'd be here now," Eden answered, her voice solemn.

"You didn't answer my question."

"You and I haven't seen each other or talked in years," Eden said, her brow furrowed. "And you walk in here and act like this."

"Answer the question," Katie barked.

"No," was Eden's response. "I will not stay away from him."

"You selfish, spoiled debutante—" Katie exploded. "You left Finn to marry a man who abused you. And now, ten years later, you grovel after Finn like a lost, sick puppy. I realize now that if Finn ever did return to you he'd be a complete moron; an idiot I'd want nothing to do with! You're pathetic."

Those verbal darts hurled at Eden couldn't penetrate. Not after all she had been through in life. "The only people who were there for me when I needed them were Joanna and my parents," Eden spoke coolly. Then she marched to the door and swung it open. "Only their opinions matter to me now. I'd like for you to leave. Now."

"You're completely messed up!" Katie screamed, storming out and whizzing past Ryan, who was carrying groceries for the next morning's breakfast.

"What's wrong?" Ryan exclaimed. Eden rushed into her bedroom.

"Eden?" Joanna called after her.

"I want to be alone!" she yelled and shut her door.

Eden rolled off her bed and switched on a lamp. She lifted a book of art, trying to distract herself by reading. That didn't work. She watched the rolling green hills drop into the sea. There, the orange and brick-red sun had always set so magnificently.

Dawn broke and another knock came from their front door.

Joanna rushed through the hall, glancing into Eden's empty room. Joanna checked the peephole again, relaxed, and opened the door for Finn. His eyes were heavy and sleepless; he opened his mouth, but no words came.

"Eden's not here," Joanna said. "Her stuff's still in her room but she isn't."

"Where is she?"

"She probably went for a walk. I'll have Ryan call you when she comes back." Finn turned and started toward his car. "When's your flight?" she yelled after him. But Finn was already in the driver's seat and closing the door.

He drove to all their special places. The beach. The coffee shop. There, the barristas were removing chairs from tabletops and returning them to their positions.

Finn slowed near Alumni Park, but she wasn't there, either. A fog had pushed into campus, clouding everything. At the lacrosse field, minutes later, Finn dimmed his car lights to penetrate the fog. He stepped out and walked to the hill's edge. Finally being able to see the green, he saw that no one stirred.

Finn returned to his apartment and threw his suitcase into the backseat and shut the door. At that moment, a sudden memory struck him. He darted into the driver's seat and sped off.

Finn arrived back at Joanna and Eden's apartment, ran across the side of the complex and to the back, where Eden's sliding glass door opened onto the porch, facing the sunrise. And there she was, wrapped in her blanket, sitting against the wall, crying into her hands.

Eden glanced up and saw him. The fresh light from daybreak illuminated his shirt. She bit her lip and swiped the tears from her cheeks and nose. Before she could move, Finn was already taking her hands and helping her to her feet.

"Finn," she whimpered, touching his cheek with her hand, making sure he was real. Finn kissed her wrist and held her hand against his face.

"I'm sorry I was harsh with you." She shook her

head and tried to speak, but Finn stopped her. "I've spent years building walls. And suddenly, you reappeared and I had to tear down those walls overnight. You wrote that you loved me. If you've changed your mind, tell me now and I'll never bother you again. But if you do love me, I should tell you there's not a man on this earth who will love you like I will. Anything you want or need, I'll provide for you if it's within my power. I swear to God, I'll love you the rest of my life."

"I love you," she said.

At those words, he lifted her into his arms and kissed her. And the sun burst forth between them.

Additional Writings

Part 1. The Missing Letter in the Mason Jar

In the first draft of *The Mason Jar*, a final letter from the grandfather was found under the broken Mason jar. That letter was originally eight pages long. At various times, portions of the letter were added to previous letters, and other portions were deleted. With Mr. Lingerfelt's permission, here is the original letter from the first draft, in full.

Dear Clayton,

I decided to go ahead and write this while it was fresh on my mind. Forgive me for its length, but I wanted to get it all out on paper so that when you returned from your visit to California, we could go over it together and discuss it.

You cannot make sense of your own story while living it. Often, things are understood only in hindsight. I know your heart is hurting, but come with me for awhile. Much of this will not be easy for you to hear. I am sure it will touch too close to your heart at times, so I encourage you to set the letter aside anytime it feels too heavy and understand that I wouldn't write these things if I didn't care about you.

Over the years I have observed certain things that continually cause pain in your life. Your inexperience due to your young age, partnered with expectations you bring to the world. In your mind, the world should be a certain way, and you tend to believe everyone sees the world as you do. Then you come face to face with reality, and you're let down. This is Realism versus Idealism.

You tend to see things in either black or white. In your mind, the answers to your questions are either "yes" or "no." In this great earth and this infinite space, all overseen by an Infinite God, do you believe that your interactions with such a life will yield easy answers and conclusions? Use your head, son. Don't push your wants so much that you ignore what experience has taught you. Trust your intuition and instincts more. Remember how small we all really are.

You also have an expectation of who God is supposed to be. You've been raised in a very religious culture, where humans have defined God through logic, reason, theology, and philosophy. Do you truly believe God can be defined or bound by any human mind? Jesus never said that a certain teaching or action summed up God.

Jesus only taught and did things that reflected who God is: a God of love and mercy but also one of judgment. These are characteristics of God, but they do not fully define Him, nor is He contained or limited by them.

What you know of God is what He has been able to convey to you through your observations and experiences within your limited capacity of understanding. These are the limitations of the finite human mind. Your mother's love, your father's instruction, your inner heart which tells you when you've done wrong, statements of truth you already know are true when you encounter them; these are what you know of God and all you can know of Him until He reveals more of Himself to you. He not only knows when to show you truth, but He knows how much you can handle. He will reveal more when you're ready.

God loves you. He is for you, not against you. He is out for our better good, even though we often do not believe it. His ideas are not our own, for His are much higher.

I've watched you passionately pursue philosophy, understanding, and romantic love without caution. That mentality has an aura of heroism, but it's foolish. When we come to the point of realizing that there are few answers and solutions in this life, we find that we are no longer obsessed with an anxious desire to control life or to find all of its answers. We then bask in the freshness of the moment, of how it feels to be fully alive, and we can then enjoy the journey.

Like most young men, you sought to understand the feminine and have placed certain expectations on her. The masculine will never understand the feminine, and that was never meant to be the masculine's objective. Through the confusion that is inevitable in growing up, we tend to lose sight of the fact that the feminine is to be loved, cherished, admired, respected, welcomed, invited, and celebrated, but never worshipped. She cannot and will never be understood; she's not supposed to be.

I once believed that we humans marry to provide stability, to combat loneliness, or to have children. Now I believe that marriage is to be chosen only so that we may love another human unconditionally and connect in a way that is impossible with anyone else. If we marry for any other reason, the bond of marriage will not be as strong. Many people marry so that they can receive love. What they receive instead are disappointed lives. We marry to offer love. When we do that, we have married for the right reason.

A theologian remarked that when the masculine joins with the feminine, the two halves of God unite and become one. The feminine is the missing element when the masculine stands alone. That's why the marital covenant is so sacred. I'm not sure what the Infinite realm is like, but that theologian wrote the description beautifully. And it keeps me in love with poetry.

This life that I am speaking of, if we are to enjoy it fully, will require a lot of letting go of things we tend to squeeze with dear might.

First, we must let go of our desire to control. Remember that the source of pain and sorrow usually begins with a naïve notion called Entitlement. This attitude of, "I am entitled to this and that." We are entitled to nothing. We entered this world with a clenched fist, and we will exit with an open hand. When we grasp this truth, much of the source of pain and sorrow in our lives will go away.

We must let go of our pride and self.

Stop asking, "How am I being treated?" In Philippians, St. Paul writes that as long as the good news of God is preached, men can do whatever they desire to him. Also, notice how Jesus was always very calm and serene in most circumstances.

We must let go of our desires to be someone important. Let us be more concerned about whether Christ's character is transforming our own. Pray for His Holy Spirit to dwell and make Himself known in your words and deeds, your character. Love people. Love has a different manner of revealing itself through each person. Expecting others to love as we do isn't realistic. Only you are you and can give and receive love the way you do. It's an adventure, too, because you discover how you and others differ in the ways you love.

And finally, let us let go of our dependency on others to shape our identity. God loves you unconditionally, so why is it that you often find your identity based on what another human thinks of you? We reject people, and people reject us. Do we not, in some form, reject strangers when we pass by them in a café or on a sidewalk and do not stop and speak to them? There simply is not enough energy in you or others to greet and show personal attention to every single person you pass on the street. Therefore, do not be ashamed when you are rejected in more intimate settings, since many of these same principles apply.

Eden was young, Clayton, and so were you. Your time together was over five years ago. She's not the same person now, and neither are you. I didn't really know your grandmother, even though we were married for thirty-seven years, because we were both always changing. Every day, you're different than the person you were yesterday. No one truly knows us. We really don't even know ourselves. Only God does.

I do believe Eden cared about you, but I'm not sure she loved you, as hard as that is to hear. If you went on a few dates, kissed, and parted, both of you knowing that your time together was an attempt to ease loneliness or better someone's self-esteem, you would have seen it for what it was, and it would not have had this strong effect on you. You have the courage to feel everything so deeply, a courage many of us lack. But because you believed she was in love with you, you returned that love, full-throttle. You not only lowered the guards around your heart, you removed them. That, I feel, is what made her parting so treacherous.

When you met Eden, I know you were still healing from things you encountered in other countries. I went through similar issues after my time in Africa. It's not easy to see human suffering face to face for the first time. You had become burnt out, and those experiences coupled with the intensity that graduate school demands spent and exhausted every bit of you. Eden entering your life was fresh water to a barren land. The relationship was graceful. She alone brought you happiness, and that's a dangerous thing, to give that kind of power to a person, because people let us down, they're human. So when she left, you plummeted lower than before you met her. This can happen when we place our identity, self-worth, or our life's trust into a human, no matter how promising the relationship seems.

It's not your fault she left, and it's not God's fault, either. As far as we know, God did bring her into your life as a potential mate, yet through her free will she chose to leave. It was Eden's decision to part, a decision based on twenty-two years of her entire life's observations and experiences combined with her personality and chemicals shaped through thousands of years of ancestry genetics manifesting themselves simultaneously in a single moment.

That's a mouthful, I know, but that's also my point. Many factors come together in the decisions we choose to make. That's the mystery of being human.

She decided to choose a boy she had known intimately through four years of sharing life together. When you're twenty-two, four years is a long time. Her emotional attachment to him was a barrier between her and you, and it prevented her from giving her entire self to you. That explains why she could act so in love with you one second and literally treat you as a stranger the next. It's why she could leave so easily without looking back.

The reason you have battled with God over all this and will continue to battle with Him for some time is faith. All of your life, especially during your later teens and early twenties, you were awarded by your giant leaps of faith and how life seemed to fall into order for you. It was not you that awarded yourself, but rather it was God rewarding your faith, thus astounding you. Eden was the first time you made a leap of faith and you were not rewarded with the gift you expected in return. When that happened, it shattered your interpretation of God's work in your past. You began to question if all those times you believed God moved in your life resulted from illusion, from cognitive dissonance (meaning, to believe something is true because we want it to be true).

No one consciously wishes to be deceived. And you need to begin introducing your heart to the possibility that your interpretations in regards to your encounter with Eden were the result of cognitive dissonance. In other words, everything made sense with Eden because subconsciously, you wanted it to make sense.

My question for you, Clayton, is that if Eden is so wonderful and wise as you have said, then why did she leave? The struggle is, "I can't live without her," versus "She's too dumb and doesn't realize what she's giving up." It's okay to feel angry, but make sure to separate her from her decision. Be angry with her decision, not her.

One day you will ask yourself, "How do I finally get over her?" And the response must be, "I must come to the place where

I will say no to her if she tries to return, and I must be at peace with this decision." Remember, in the world, we choose our friends. In God, He chooses our friends for us, and we choose whether or not to like them. Once your emotions settle and you get over her—and you will get over her—you will then be able to reflect on your time together at Pepperdine and see moments, signs that Eden was not the woman you thought she was.

As time passes, it will dawn in your mind concretely that if you and Eden were meant to be together, then she would have never left, not even for a moment. You will realize that you placed Eden on your own hand-crafted pedestal and that your interpretations of your encounters with her are actually very different than the encounters themselves. The answers were always there, but you were too blinded by love and emotion, no matter how often you deny emotion's influence in your life. You'll then be able to remove her from the pedestal you crafted for her and find peace in saying goodbye to a girl you barely knew.

You have the ability now to put the past behind you. You don't need to contact Eden anymore. Let her be. Sometimes, that is the greatest way we can love someone: just let them be. This is your chance to prove to yourself your own strength, character, and integrity by caring for someone romantically yet sacrificing those feelings for her better good, by staying away from her. This will be the test of real love for you. Desire the best for her. Let her live her life in peace without knowing the hurt she caused you.

We must love people enough to enrich our lives while we have them, but not give them so much power that they impoverish our lives when they are gone. Our grief and pain are directly proportional to our love. The depth and level of pain are proof that we loved. And anytime we choose to love anyone, there is the risk that such love will not be returned. Despite the lies you will tell yourself, life is more fulfilling and worthy of living if we love and lose than if we never love at all.

One day you will withdraw your emotional energy from Eden and reinvest it into another relationship. When this happens, do not think that you are turning your back on the one you loved. Loving others does not mean that you love the first love any less, but it recognizes that there are other people who need our love. In the loss of a close relationship, it should be suspicious if any full resolution takes under a year. For some people, two years isn't enough. Five years isn't too long, either. What matters is whether or not the healing is occurring. Here, I am attaching a piece of literature I came across years ago which I think will help you.

Many people misunderstand this task and therefore need help with it, especially in the case of the death of a spouse. They think that if they withdraw their emotional attachment, they are somehow dishonoring the memory of the deceased. In some cases they are frightened by the prospect of reinvesting their emotions in another relationship because it too might end with a loss and be taken from them. Others have the romantic notion that they are married for life and therefore cannot ever love another. It is difficult to find a phrase that adequately defines the incompletion of this task, but I think the best description would perhaps be not loving. This task is hindered by holding on to the past attachment rather than going on and forming new ones. Some people find loss so painful that they make a pact with themselves never to love again. The popular song market is replete with this theme, which gives it a validity it does not deserve.

In the beginning, all seems grand until we experience the desert. This is much like the Israelites who had lentils and lamb back in Egypt and complained when they were fed only bread in the wilderness. Oh, if they had only known what was awaiting them in the Promised Land. Oftentimes in life, just before things get better, just before we reach Acceptance and Peace and the Promised Land, we grow cynical and bitter because we still find ourselves in the lull, and we think that this is the best life will get, that it will never be like it once was. That is when most people give up and turn to a life of resentment and bitterness. Some will even commit suicide.

If a person has never been cut, they might believe that the wound will only heal to a bloody scab. What they don't know or understand is that eventually that scab will turn into a scar whose wound no longer hurts. We remember our wounds by the scars we keep, but they are no longer painful. This takes time, and we are not in control of Time's speed.

It's hard to remember or hope for sunshine when all you find is darkness around you. But remember the good times from the past, and let those memories provide hope for what lies ahead. There is always a sense of sadness when we think of the people we loved and lost, but it's a different kind of sadness. As time passes, it lacks the wrenching inner-twisting it once had. You will know that you are coming to a place of healing when you think on your loss without pain.

Let me say one more thing before I bring this letter to a close. Remember we become what our minds dwell on. It's proven in cognitive psychology that if we dwell on negative thoughts, we become negative people. "A man reaps what he sows," so said St. Paul. If we live in the past, in a world that we cannot change, we only grow estranged from the present. We stop growing and decay. If the past brings good memories, let them brighten your present day, but do not long for their return or dwell on them. For it is the present day that must be taken care of if we are to expect to live fruitfully tomorrow. It is true that understanding our past helps us understand ourselves, but also remember that we are shaped by our past—not bound by it.

Examine the words you tell yourself, and eliminate thoughts of anger, negativity, and resentment. "Think on what is noble, right, pure, lovely, admirable, the things that are excellent and praiseworthy," so said St. Paul. You still have your health; you have two legs, two eyes, and two ears that work properly. You do not have to worry about returning to your house and wondering if it will be burned because a neighboring town hated your community. You never have to fear coming home to a butchered family because of tribal wars. You have a bed to sleep in every night, you have winter and summer clothing, and you've always been provided with three meals a day. Most importantly, you have two parents, an older brother, and a grandfather who would give their lives so that you might simply live a happy one.

Think on the importance of being and living, enjoying and loving all that exists, visible and invisible, and don't miss its beauties. Think daily on the things you are thankful for. Do not miss them. They are like kisses from God, inviting us to enjoy the life that surrounds us.

As I leave you, our role in this world might be small, but it is very important. Take heart. If you decide to return to Africa, I'll understand. I've been there, and I know how a place like that can grab hold of you and refuse to let go. Vanderbilt will be there when you're ready.

One day, son, you will find a group of older, wise, and experienced men, professors, missionaries, leaders from local non-profits to counsel you. Pray with them, and share your inner struggles and rejoices with the ones you trust. Find close friends who've served as missionaries, humanitarians, counselors, and pastors. Drink coffee and tea with them as I know you will. There, you will laugh, enjoy their presence, and hear their own confessions of wrong-doing, mourning, and pleas for forgiveness. You will be a rope for them in times of weakness, and they will be a rope for you.

You will find joy again, very similar to the joy you possessed when you were a boy. But it will be a different kind of joy. It will be a sober joy. The melancholy you have felt these years may never leave. But its volume will be turned down low. You will never throw yourself into self-pity again, and you will find peace. In the words of an old church hymn, "What lies in tomorrow? I don't know. It might bring me poverty. But the one who feeds the sparrow is the one who stands by me. There are many things about tomorrow that I don't understand, but I know who holds tomorrow, and I know who holds my hand."

Just as the sky turns a faint pink in the early morning, when you desire to reinvest your life into an intimate, confessional relationship with another, that is evidence that the sun is rising and that the earth is warming. No cloud stays around forever. There is always a spring, and even in the winter months, the sun manages to shine on occasional days.

You've stumbled, you've fallen, but despite all you've been through, you've always picked yourself back up and leaned on God. At the end of every day, no matter what happens, you still say to Him, "Your will be done—not mine." And that is to be commended.

I love you, son.

—Grandpa

Part 2. A Deleted Chapter

The night before Mr. Lingerfelt's book was sent to the printer, he deleted this final chapter from the memoir which Clayton Fincannon wrote. Mr. Lingerfelt felt the book would have a stronger punch with Finn boarding the plane to Africa, rather than these final words from Finn. With Mr. Lingerfelt's permission, here is that chapter.

"I am not so poor: I can smell the ripening apples; the very rills are deep; the autumnal flowers, the *trichostema dichotomum*—not only its bright blue flower above the sand, but its strong wormwood scent which belongs to the season, feed my spirit, endear the earth to me, make me value myself and rejoice; the quivering of pigeon's wings reminds me of the tough fiber of the air which they rend. Thank you, God. I do not deserve anything, I am unworthy of the least regard; and yet I am made to rejoice. I am pure and worthless, and yet the world is gilded for my delight and holidays are prepared for me, and my path is strewn with flowers."

—Henry D. Thoreau,
The Heart of Thoreau's Journals

I have tried my best to sift through the thoughts my heart makes of my experiences. I can hardly say that today or tomorrow life will ever make sense. When I stand before our Creator to give an account of my life, with all my well thought-out philosophical ideas and teachings concerning the meaning of life and its poetry and music we write with our lives, I believe He'll pat me on the back and smile, saying, "Well, son, it was a noble effort." And I will wink at the questions I pursued while I lived on Earth, finally understanding how limited my mind really was.

The philosopher I once tried to be is no longer. These days I instead prefer poetry and the company of loved ones. Chesterton was right when he said it's chess players, not poets, who go insane. I never stop learning. I still have questions, and I know that most will be answered only in the next life. Questions ache the brain, but love warms the heart, and I much prefer the latter.

When I think on God, I see He knows the intimate stories of every single human being who has ever lived on the planet. Though there is pain in everyone's life, there is so much beauty. Everyone has a story and God knows all of them. I imagine Him to be very romantic.

Do I still love Eden? I think a part of me will always love Eden, just as I love all the people from my past. Though there are some people who I haven't seen or spoken to in years, it doesn't mean I don't think about them. And it doesn't mean I don't love them.

When I am old and what hair is left has turned white, when the strength of youth is gone, and all of my memories have been made sweet and lovely due to the passing of time, I believe inner peace will be as familiar to me as sliding my feet into my slippers.

I will walk along the pastures and fields of our farm on an autumn afternoon, among the leaves that have changed from green to orange to reds and almonds. I will pass the little cafés and shop windows near our home and see a reflection of a man resembling a boy I once knew. An elderly man will stare back at me in his overcoat and hat who taps the sidewalk with his umbrella at every other step.

The breeze will scatter the leaves as my memories come alive, and I'll remember a time in college when I was young and passionate and life was new. I will remember Eden: the first time we embraced at the beach, the night I walked her to her car as she hesitated about leaving, her mother and father smiling at me from across their welcoming table, Eden and I dancing in my bedroom and sipping wine on Valentine's, and the graduation party at the president's house where she shook my chin and said I looked scruffy.

My thoughts will be interrupted by my grandson, running up to me with a headful of questions. And for some reason, that will make me smile. I will have a Mason jar on my desk, and if he chooses to leave a letter for me, that will be just fine. He knows a response will await him, when he is ready. He will inquire about what life was like when I was his age, and I will chuckle and ask him if he wants the long version or the short one.

I will tell him education is not only in books, but in serving and spending time with people. I will tell him to remind himself daily that death comes to us all and to keep his life in a proper perspective. I will tell him to show compassion to the people beside him no matter the circumstances, whether they are his friend or foe, to live a life out of thankfulness for the love God has shown us instead of thinking we must earn His love. God loves us no matter our past, our present, or our future, and we must stop imagining that God will love us when we become the people we should be, because we'll never be the people we should be.

I will tell him happiness is a mindset, we are only rich and poor based on who we compare ourselves to. Love really is the most powerful action on earth, and if practiced unconditionally, can bring meaning to a life that's broken and torn. I will tell him true life is found in submitting our entire lives to God's will, that sometimes He says no, not because He's angry with us, but because if

He had said yes, we would have strayed further off course.

And I will tell him that no matter how many crosses we must bear or how many days, weeks, months, or even years we spend in the tomb, Easter Sunday will come. The sun will shine again. And in our hearts, whether we care to admit it or not, we and God are romantic.

High School Teacher Guide

PART I

1. Who do we meet and where?
2. Where does she work?
3. What is a curator?
4. Where is Eden originally from?
5. How long has she been here?
6. Who is Joanna and why does she call Eden?
7. Who is Clayton Fincannon?
8. What is the book about that Fincannon has written?
9. Why do you think Eden is so "distracted" by the idea of Fincannon's book?
10. Based on what you read in Part I, what do you think Fincannon's book will be about?

Chapter 1

1. What season is it?
2. Describe Finn's grandpa.
3. What is a mentor?
4. Why was Grandpa a mentor to Finn?
5. As Finn begins to tell his story of Eden, where is the setting?

6. Who introduced Finn and Eden?
7. What is Finn studying in graduate school? And Eden?
8. What does Finn wear on this first date?
9. Based on how Finn describes Eden, the evening, and what he wears, what do you think his expectations are?
10. What does it seem that both Finn and Eden are interested in?
11. Where do Finn and Eden go together the next day?
12. Who is Eden's favorite artist and why?
13. What does Finn compare Eden's speech to?
14. What does Finn ask Eden to do about their relationship? Why?
15. Where do they go on this second date?
16. What does Finn say that traveling alone does for you?
17. How does Finn feel about Eden at the end of Chapter 1?
18. Is it wise that Finn feels this way?

Chapter 2

1. What are some activities that Eden and Finn do together the next few days?
2. What does Eden share with Finn about her family?
3. What special day in Eden's life approaches?

4. What does she ask of Finn? What is his response?
5. Where do Eden and Finn go before leaving Malibu?
6. Tell about Oz's background.
7. Why is Finn called "Finn"?
8. What are Eden's memories of Colorado?
9. What is similar about Eden's and Finn's youth?
10. What is different about their lives?

Chapter 3

1. Who picks them up at the airport?
2. What does Finn stop to buy?
3. What type of house do they live in?
4. When did Mr. and Mrs. Valmont meet?
5. Where does Eden go during dinner?
6. What does Finn tell Mrs. Valmont that he has learned through his experiences?
7. How old is Eden today?
8. How long do Eden and Finn stay in Colorado?
9. Who does Finn call the next day to find out about Eden?
10. How long have Eden and Finn known each other at this point?
11. What surprising fact do we learn at the end of the chapter?

Chapter 4

1. Why does Finn believe Eden left him?
2. What does Finn compare her leaving to and what does the comparison mean?
3. Finn says, "Life always makes sense when you're home." What do you think Finn means by this? What feelings does "home" connotate?
4. What do you think it means that Finn immediately begins reliving his time at home? How do these nostalgic feelings play into his getting over Eden?
5. What do you think Grandpa means by saying that "love is action . . . a decision . . . self-sacrifice"? What do you think about this definition of love?
6. Explain the symbolism behind Grandpa's story about Birdie.
7. What has Grandpa left for Finn in the Mason jar?
8. Finn ends this chapter by saying, "Life's easier when you're quiet." Based on what has happened to him over the past two weeks, what does he mean?

PART II

1. What new insight do we have into Eden's life?
2. How did Eden assume Finn felt about her?

Chapter 5

1. How is life at Pepperdine now for Finn?
2. Who is Dr. Daniels?
3. What does Dr. Daniels propose Finn do for the summer?
4. Why does Finn ask Grandpa if he ever struggled with loneliness?
5. Grandpa compares Finn's troubles to Christ's suffering on Friday saying that "we are Easter people." Research the meaning of Easter and then explain what Grandpa means.
6. What does Finn decide to do?

Chapter 6

1. Who goes to Africa with Finn?
2. What does William say Finn will be helping with in Africa?
3. Why do you think Finn isn't afraid of Africa?

4. In Finn's dream, how does he respond to Eden's attempted apology? What does this teach you about forgiveness?
5. Describe the mood in the jazz club. What does this mood reflect about Finn's inner thoughts?

Chapter 7

1. Where is Finn's first stop and the reason?
2. What do they eat?
3. What is a house warming and who has one and how does it go?
4. Finn says you can tell a lot about a person by the greatest compliment he ever received. Why do you think this is true? What is your greatest compliment and what does it say about you?
5. Who is Bernard and what does Finn talk to him about?
6. At the end of Finn's journal, why do you think he says he would like to be more like the shepherd boys?
7. Why does Finn feel guilty for having the trail mix?
8. Why do Finn and Jimmy befriend the Ugandan man on the bus?

Chapter 8

1. Where is Finn staying now?
2. What is the daily routine at the boys' center?
3. What is Saturday night at the orphanage?
4. How old do the boys have to be to stay at the farm?
5. When Finn looks at the picture of him and Eden, what is he reminded of?
6. What is in Eastleigh?
7. Describe Taylor and her relationship with Finn. Why is Finn sorry for the pain he caused her?

PART III

1. What do we discover about Finn's letters to Eden?

Chapter 9

1. Why did the missionaries give the street boys a sewing machine?
2. Based on what you read, write out the basic principles of microlending.
3. How long does Finn stay in Nairobi?

Chapter 10

1. Who wants to see Finn at the U.S. Embassy?
2. What does Duncan want of Finn? Why does he choose Finn?
3. What does Finn decide?

Chapter 11

1. After Finn returns home, who calls and what does he want?
2. What do you think Finn means by "you take yourself with you"?
3. What is the theme of Finn's letter to Grandpa?
4. What does Grandpa suggest Finn do and does he follow through?
5. What does Eden's mother tell Finn?

Chapter 12

1. Based on what Finn shares with Ryan, what is Finn feeling? Why?
2. How do you feel about what Finn wrote in his journal at the end of the chapter? Do you agree with it? What is Finn really trying to say?

Chapter 13

1. What has happened to Grandpa?
2. How do you think Finn feels now that he got the news about Eden?

Chapter 14

1. What does Finn do next?
2. How does Caleb feel about his brother leaving again?

**What if the story ended here? Write another ending before reading Part IV, using the same characters and circumstances.

PART IV

1. How do you think Eden feels after having read Finn's book about their time together so many years ago?
2. Why does Eden call her dad?
3. How does Eden feel about Finn at this point?
4. When Eden is at the first gathering at the reunion, where does she see Finn?
5. Why is Finn rude to Eden?

6. Have Finn's feelings for Eden changed by the way he speaks to her at the banquet?
7. What happens before Finn catches his flight?
8. Hypothesize about what would happen if Finn had said no to Eden and returned home. What kind of life would he have lived? What about her?

FOLLOW-UP

1. Explain the significance of the Mason jar in the title and throughout the story.
2. In 3-4 pages, extend the story after Eden and Finn meet at the lacrosse game using the same characters and circumstances.
3. If Finn had to live his life over and never wrote the book or journeyed back to Pepperdine for his reunion, thus never seeing Eden again, do you think he would avoid Eden or experience her love all over again? What do you base your decision on? How would Finn's life be different if he had never met Eden? Be specific.
5. Research Caravaggio's life, time period, culture, and work. Write a 3-4 page paper detailing his life and accomplishments. Also include how/why he is connected with this book.

6. Read The Missing Letter under Additional Writings. In your own words, what is the overall message of the letter? Which portions stood out to you the most?

7. What does Finn's deleted chapter reveal about how he has changed?

8. Explain why Finn chooses to include the quote from Thoreau.

9. Research Henry David Thoreau's life, time period, culture, and writings. Write a 3-4 page paper detailing his life and accomplishments. Also include how/why he is connected with this book.

10. Since Christianity is a theme throughout the book, research its origin, leaders, and foundations of belief. Write this up in a 3-4 page formal research paper.

James Russell Lingerfelt
currently divides his time between
Tennessee and Southern California.

Learn more at www.jamesrussell.org